Great Britain Laws

The Small Holdings Act

1892 - and the statutory provisions incorporated therein

Great Britain Laws

The Small Holdings Act
1892 - and the statutory provisions incorporated therein

ISBN/EAN: 9783337403768

Printed in Europe, USA, Canada, Australia, Japan

Cover: Foto ©Andreas Hilbeck / pixelio.de

More available books at **www.hansebooks.com**

The Small Holdings Act,

1892,

AND THE

STATUTORY PROVISIONS

INCORPORATED THEREIN.

BY

HORACE E. MILLER, LL.B.,

Of the Middle Temple and South-Eastern Circuit, Barrister-at-Law;
Joint Author of STEPHEN *and* MILLER'S *"County Council Compendium."*

TOGETHER WITH A

PREFACE

BY THE

RIGHT HON. JESSE COLLINGS, M.P.

LONDON:

WATERLOW AND SONS LIMITED, LONDON WALL,

1892.

TABLE OF CONTENTS.

THE

AGRICULTURAL HOLDINGS (ENGLAND) ACT, 1883,

WITH NOTES AND FORMS, AND A SUMMARY OF
THE PROCEDURE,

BY

J. W. JEUDWINE,

Of Lincoln's Inn, Barrister-at-Law.

Second Edition.   In Cloth, 3/6.

AUTHOR'S NOTE.

THIS book is the result of an attempt to place in the hands of those who are likely to become purchasers or tenants under the Small Holdings Act (as well as members of County Councils and of the legal profession) a ready means of reference to the provisions of that important measure. Opportunity has been taken in the Introduction to discuss various matters which have been deemed essential to a complete grasp of the chief features of the subject.

The Author desires to call the attention of members of County Councils to the difficulty of the question whether the Councils shall let land on hire or insist upon a purchase. The main object of the Small Holdings Act is the restoration of a class of society once of great consequence in this country, viz., the yeomen. But although this is so, it will not be politic to discourage the mere hiring of land under the Act ; nor should persons offering to hire land from a Council be subjected to any examination *as to their ability to become purchasers hereafter.* It may easily happen that persons will offer to hire by way of experiment, being unwilling to risk their savings at first upon a purchase. County Councils will do well to construe the provisions of the Act liberally, and to consider very fully whether the land should be let or sold outright.

The Author gladly acknowledges his obligations to the Right Hon. Jesse Collings, M.P., who has not only supplied much valuable information, but has also, at the Author's request, written an interesting Preface.

1, GARDEN COURT, TEMPLE, E.C.,
   September 14*th*, 1892.

PREFACE.

THE following pages contain a clear and comprehensive exposition of an Act of Parliament which, from a social as well as from an economic point of view, may be regarded as one of the most important that has been passed during the present generation.

The Small Holdings Act, if judiciously and generally administered, will benefit directly or indirectly the whole rural population. It will open up to the agricultural labourers especially prospects and opportunities of a career on the land which they have not hitherto had, and will go far to alter the dead level of their lives, which drives so many of them—particularly the young—to seek other occupations.

There are those who hold that the State has no right to give assistance to any class of men to " help

them in their business." However generally sound
this principle might be, it has no application in the
case of workers on the land. The depopulation of
our country-sides, and consequent overcrowding of our
cities and towns, are sources of grave national danger.
The decay of its rural population is the greatest evil
that can befall a country. A nation might attain
a position of wealth and greatness by commercial
enterprise, but history shows that its permanence,
solidity, and resisting power are mainly dependent
on and bound up with a numerous and settled population of the peasant class. On the grounds of national
good and national security, therefore, an experiment
is warranted, is an act of good statesmanship, which
has for its object to restore and increase the prosperity
of the village life.

Besides this, a debt is due to the agricultural
labourers as a class. The operation of the Inclosure
Acts, which from 1760 to 1844 inclosed such a large
part of the land of England, while securing great
benefits to the nation as a whole, was at the same time
injurious to the peasantry as a class. It brought land
into cultivation, increased and improved enormously—

both per acre and in the aggregate—the supply of corn, cattle, and other food, and led to great progress in agriculture generally. On the other hand, these inclosures and the general practice of consolidation of holdings which ensued were causes which, combined, led to the severance of the peasantry from the land, and reduced them to the position of mere wage receivers. On this ground alone the labourers of to-day, the descendants and representatives of the peasantry of former generations, would seem to have a moral claim on the nation, a claim which is wisely recognised in the present Act. As to the economic principle involved in the experiment, experience in other countries proves it to be a sound one. The main object of the Act is that of " cultivating ownership." The Government wisely resisted all attempts to turn the measure into one for the creation of small " tenancies," with the County Councils as landlords, a system which would have been foredoomed to failure.

By the gradual increase of small holdings created under the Act it might reasonably be expected that more and more of the smaller articles of food, for which we pay so many millions annually to foreign countries, will be produced at home. In "peasant proprietorship" alone can be found the conditions most suitable for the successful production of these articles of food. These conditions are hard work, close personal attention to small things, moderate gains, together with the security and independence which belong to the position. On this economic side of the question may be quoted the great authority of Adam Smith, who says: "A small proprietor, who " knows every part of his little territory, who views " it with all the affection which property, especially " small property, naturally inspires, and who upon that " account takes pleasure not only in cultivating but in " adorning it, is generally of all improvers the most " industrious, the most intelligent, and the most " successful."

JESSE COLLINGS.

EDGBASTON, BIRMINGHAM,
  September, 1892.

The Small Holdings Act,

1892.

INTRODUCTION.

IT is now about ten years since the question of obtaining a wider distribution of the land among the people of this country, by means not open to the many and serious objections to which the so-called " socialistic " doctrines relating to the land are liable, was first brought forward as a matter worthy of the immediate attention of Parliament. The honour of being the pioneer in this good work falls, beyond question, to the lot of the Rt. Hon. member for the Bordesley Division, Mr. Jesse Collings. But although proposals of a practical character were first made by him in the parliamentary session of 1881, and repeated in the sessions of the years following, the only forward step taken, as regards legislation, between the years 1881 and 1887, was in the passing of the Allotments Extension Act, 1882 (45 & 46 Vict. c. 80), which was promoted by Mr. Collings. By the fourth section of this Act, all trustees in whom lands are vested, or by whom they are held or managed for the benefit of the poor of any parish or place in or adjoining that where such lands are situate, and of which the rents or produce are distributed in gifts of money, doles, fuel, clothing, bread, or other articles of sustenance or necessity, are required (whenever such lands are not otherwise used for the general benefit or enjoyment of the inhabitants) to render available for allotments the said lands or such portion thereof as the demand may necessitate. The Act applies to all charity lands, except those used for educational, ecclesiastical, and apprenticeship purposes, and contains all subsidiary provisions calculated to secure the due execution of this section ; and, although it deals only with charity lands, yet these lands occupy, in the whole, so large an area, that the Act has been the means of providing allotments for a good many thousands of labourers.

Perseverance, however, had its wonted result, for in the session of 1887 the Government undertook to legislate with respect to allotments, the first branch of the subject, and passed the Act of that year, which, it is well known, is of general application. This Act has, it is believed, been of great benefit to many who desired to have plots of ground for cultivation, and has added many thousands to the previous number of allotments, which had been created under the Inclosure Acts, or the Act of 1882, or by private action and enterprise, and of which, in 1886, there were 357,795 in Great Britain.

The local executive authority, for the purposes of the Allotments Act of 1887, was the sanitary authority, *i.e.*, in the rural districts, the Board of Guardians. The only other local authority to which, at this time, the administration of the Act could have been entrusted was the Quarter Sessions, upon which it was not, however, deemed expedient to impose this duty. A good many of the Boards of Guardians being found unwilling to put the Act into force, a remedy was provided in the amending Act of 1890. By this measure, whenever the local authority refuses or neglects to exercise its powers under the Act of 1887, a memorial may be addressed by six or more ratepayers in a district to the County Council by way of substitution for the local sanitary authority. Hereupon it becomes the duty of the County Council to appoint an Allotments Committee, by whom inquiries must be made; and the Council, if satisfied by the inquiry that land for allotments should be acquired, must then pass a resolution to that effect, and thereupon the powers and duties of the sanitary authority under the Act of 1887 are *transferred* from the sanitary authority to the County Council, by whom the provisions of the Act are thereafter to be executed. The Act of 1890 has been put into force on a good many occasions since it passed, with excellent results.

The first branch of the subject being well initiated by these measures, it then remained to attempt the solution of the more difficult problems arising under the heading of small holdings; and, to this end, the Government, in the year 1888, appointed a Select

History of
the subject. Committee to inquire into the whole subject of small
holdings.   Over that Committee the Right Hon.
Joseph Chamberlain, M.P., presided.   After hearing a
great deal of evidence from persons of all shades of
opinion, this Committee ultimately reported strongly
in favour of legislation upon the subject of small
holdings.   In the session of 1892, therefore, a Government Bill was brought forward and introduced into
the House of Commons by the Right Hon. Henry
Chaplin, M.P., President of the Board of Agriculture.
That Bill embodied many provisions similar to those
contained in the Bill which for many sessions Mr.
Collings had brought before Parliament, and the
Government Bill therefore received the most careful
attention and the most loyal support at the hands of
that well-known friend of the rural population.   The
Bill, after undergoing some important modifications, as
well as acquiring some noteworthy additions, passed
both Houses and became law on the 27th of June last.

Objects of
the new
legislation   Now, however various may be the opinions enter-
tained by different people with respect to the merits
of this new legislation, it cannot be doubted that, in
the Small Holdings Act of 1892, we have one of the
most interesting attempts to grapple with a great
social question ever made by a legislative assembly.
The Act provides for the wants of various classes of
the rural population : first, a small quantity of land
for the numerous class of labourers, villagers, trades-
men, and others who are engaged, or partially engaged,
in other occupations; and next, larger holdings
suitable for those whose sole occupation is the culti-

vation of the soil. It is hoped by the promoters of the new legislation that, in the course of time, results of great practical value will be gained. The Act, while securing every advantage which can be claimed for *tenancy*, gives, at the same time, the absolute security of ownership. It offers every inducement for the exercise of that industry, energy, and thrift which history shows us to have been the great characteristics of a peasant proprietary. The objects of the Act are : (1) By means of *cultivating ownership*, and by a large increase in the amount of labour employed, to augment the productive power of the land, and thereby to benefit the manufacturing industries of the country, and, in short, to add to the national prosperity; (2) by providing the rural population with an open career on the land, to check the depopulation of the rural districts, as also the overcrowding of the labour market in towns, and the grave social evils which result from both.

These great leading purposes were well set forth in the House of Commons by Mr. Chaplin, who, when introducing the Bill, said: "One of the chief objects " we have in view is the wider distribution of land " among the people of this country ; to bring back " upon the soil, if it be possible by legislation—I had " almost said to re-create, if I may be allowed to use " the term—a class of the community which has been " gradually dwindling for many years and is now " rapidly becoming extinct, but which we must remem- " ber existed, and not only existed, but flourished in " this country in former days in far greater numbers

Objects of the new legislation.

Objects of the new legislation.

" than is the case at present, and which I am persuaded " all sections of the House of Commons would desire, " if possible, to see maintained. I am speaking now " of the class which used to be described as yeomen, " or, in other words, owners of small holdings of land. " . . . There are many other reasons which have " guided us in our decision. I will begin by mention- " ing one in particular. No one who is well acquainted " with the agricultural districts of the country can fail " to be aware of that constant migration of the rural " population from the country to the towns, which has " been so prominent and unwelcome a feature of the " rural situation during the last few years, and which I " am afraid it is true is still progressing at perhaps " an even accelerated pace to-day."

Summary of the new Act.

I pass now from these preliminary observations to take a general view of the statutory provisions which have been adopted, as being those best calculated to bring about (so far as any legislation can) the results to which reference has been made.

Executive authority.

First, as to the authority to be entrusted with the execution of the Small Holdings Act. After much consideration, it has been decided that the County Coun- cil—being the only elective body having wide powers in the rural districts—is the local authority most com- petent to undertake the work. This conclusion would have held just as good if District Councils and Parish Councils had already been constituted by Act of Par- liament and the new scheme of local autonomy thus made complete, for the County Council, besides being representative of the whole county, possesses powers

to levy rates and raise money the like of which cannot Executive authority.
be conferred upon a District Council, far less upon a
Parish Council. No statute like the Small Holdings
Act could ever be effectively worked by any Parish
Council; and this observation applies with special force
to those small, poor, and thinly-populated parishes
where the Act is likely to be most beneficial in its
operation.

It is accordingly provided that the County Council
(which term includes the council of a county-borough :
sec. 20) shall be the local authority for the purposes of
the Act.

The first duty of the County Council will be to con- Discretion of County Council as to operation of Act.
sider whether there is such a demand for small holdings
in the county that they are justified in putting the Act
into operation. To this end the Council is to appoint
a Committee to consider whether the circumstances of Committee.
the county justify an exercise of the powers of the
Act: *sec.* 5. Besides this consideration of the circumstances, the Committee are to pay all due attention to
any petition, which has been presented by any county
elector or electors, asking that the Act may be put into
operation. If the Committee find that the petition is Finding of Committee as to petition.
reasonable and made in good faith, they are forth-
with to cause a local inquiry to be made, and to report
the result of the same to the County Council. The
councillor representing, and any alderman resident in,
the district where there is said to be a demand for
small holdings are (if not already members) to be
added to the Committee: *sec.* 5.

Any such demand having been found to be a proper

2

Purchase and lease by Council. one, the County Council may then purchase land suitable for small holdings ; or if the land, owing to proximity to a town or other special reason, has a prospective value which makes purchase unadvisable or impracticable, the Council may obtain land on lease or hire : sec. 2. The Lands Clauses Acts, other than the " compulsory clauses," are applied to the purposes of the Act, together with sec. 178 of the Public Health Act, 1875.

Letting clause. The second section of the Act, which deals with letting, was an amendment moved by Mr. Collings and accepted by the Government. It applies only to land too high in price to purchase. But the object of the Act being to create, if possible, a race of cultivating owners, the County Council is intended to purchase outright, except in the special cases with which sec. 2 deals.

The Act contemplates that the Council will exercise its discretion to the best of its ability as to the question whether land shall be purchased, leased or hired. It should, however, be noted that, besides the circumstances for which sec. 2 provides, there are the restrictions imposed by sec. 18, viz., that a Council is only to acquire land at a price which will enable the Council to recoup the cost of acquisition and making the land available for holdings out of the purchase-money or rent ; and furthermore, the charge for the time being upon the county rate must not exceed in any one year the amount produced by a rate of a penny in the £.

Compulsory purchase. With regard to the question of compulsory acquisition, it was felt that there was nothing in the present

circumstances which called for the adoption of com- Compulsory
pulsory powers of purchase. There is a great deal of purchase.
land in the market; and the arguments which were
available, when considering the question of compulsory
purchase as regards allotments, were not thought to
apply, at least at this stage, to the same question as
applied to small holdings. The latter are much greater
in area, and do not involve, as allotments have often
done, the necessity of taking choice pieces of land in
the immediate neighbourhood of a town or village.
If, however, experience show them to be essential,
powers of compulsory purchase can easily be enacted.

The fourth clause of section 4 is worthy of special Holdings
worked on
notice and consideration. It runs thus : " The County co-operative
system.
" Council shall have power to sell, or, in the case of
" small holdings which may be let, to let, one or more
" small holdings to a number of persons working on a
" co-operative system, provided such system be approved
" by the County Council." This provision, which owes
its origin to the efforts of Mr. Collings, is expected to
play a conspicuous part in the practical working of the
Act, for it will enable a number of persons to unite
their means and capacities—which may easily be of a
varied character—for the advantage of each and all.
The effect of the concluding sentence of the clause is
that the persons who avail themselves of the powers
conferred by the clause will have to go to work under
rules which have received the sanction of the County
Council.

I pause here for the purpose of noting the limitations Borrowing
powers of
placed by the Act upon the power of a County Council Council.

Borrowing
powers of
Council.

to spend or borrow money for the purposes of the Act. A Council can only acquire land at a price which will allow of their recouping the expenses of acquisition, adaptation, and sale out of the purchase-money paid to the Council : *sec.* 18.

With respect to borrowing, the Council is empowered to obtain a loan from the Public Works Loans Commissioners at the rate of not less than $3\frac{1}{8}$ per centum per annum, such loan being repayable within any period not exceeding fifty years as the Local Government Board may, in each case, determine : *sec.* 19. Moreover,

Limit of
liability.

in no case is the financial liability of the Council for the purposes of the Act, including the yearly payments in respect of the loans raised, to exceed in any one year the amount produced by a rate of a penny in the £ : *sec.* 18. The effect of this limit will be better understood if it be added that the amount which a rate of a penny in the £ would produce in England and Scotland, exclusive of London and the county boroughs, would be about £10,000,000.

With regard to the percentage at which money is to be borrowed, it is important to note that, although the Public Works Loans Commissioners are not to lend at a rate lower than $3\frac{1}{8}$ per centum per annum, there is nothing in the Small Holdings Act which forbids a County Council to get the money elsewhere. Having regard to the property, funds, and rating powers of the County Councils, they will no doubt find themselves able to borrow the money required for the purposes of the Act at something less than $3\frac{1}{8}$ per cent., probably at 3 or $2\frac{3}{4}$ per cent.

The County Council have full powers, at their dis- Preparation of land. cretion, to subdivide, fence off, and otherwise carry out works which can be more economically and efficiently executed for the land as a whole. It is believed, however, that the holders will often be found able to make fences, roads, &c., more cheaply than the Council. The Council may, furthermore, erect proper Buildings on the holdings. buildings, or adapt those already standing on the land acquired, " as part of the agreement for the sale or letting of a small holding : " *sec.* 3. These works are to be executed when the Council deems them to be necessary for the due occupation of the holding, and when they cannot be carried out by the purchaser or tenant himself.

The land being thus made available and the cost, Sale and letting of holdings. rights of way and other easements, rights of grazing, &c., apportioned among the holdings, the next step will be to offer them for sale ; but if candidates for holdings are found to have inadequate means for a purchase, the Council may *let* a holding of not more than fifteen acres in extent, or, if more, of a value not exceeding £15 yearly : *sec.* 4.

The Council is to the best of its ability and discretion to apportion the total cost of acquisition, adaptation (including the expense of any works executed by the Council) and registration among the holdings into which the land required has been cut up, and then to offer them for sale or letting. There are three ways of doing this—(1) to advertise for offers in the nature of tenders ; (2) to sell or let by public auction or (3) by private contract. The last will apply when

Sale and letting of holdings. the Council have already received specific offers to purchase or hire. As already stated, a County Council is not to provide small holdings for a section of the community at the expense of the whole, but is, as far as possible, to fix the price at a sum which will cover the expenses. It may happen that the price fixed will on some occasions be a little more or less than the actual cost. Some holdings may prove to be vendible at a price higher than their actual cost, while others will go at less than actual cost, or, may be, not at all. A County Council is not, however, to provide small holdings as a commercial speculation for gain.

An important point arises as to the mode of selection of purchasers and tenants. As regards the selection of purchasers, there seems to be nothing to prevent a Council from selling to the highest bidder, as well as acting on the familiar plan of " First come, first served." But, in dealing with cases of *letting*, the Council, being without the money security which exists in the case of sale and purchase, will be under the necessity of establishing some rule of selection, and will find it essential to have special regard to the personal qualifications of the persons wishing to become tenants. Payment of rent in advance may have to be required. It seems probable that the Council may, in some cases, experience difficulty in saving itself from loss upon this point.

The seventh section of the Act specially empowers the Council to make rules for the proper conduct of sales and lettings, and also to ensure that all holdings are acquired by fit and proper persons. Here again Regulation of holdings. the Council has an unfettered discretion.

This power of *letting* holdings is a special provision Power to let holdings made in favour of those who, although wishing to become cultivating owners, are at present unable to purchase, but who, it is hoped, will in the long run be able to pay the purchase-money. The leading principle of the Act is to establish cultivating owner-ships, and every attempt to make the Act a series of provisions for creating *tenancies* was steadily resisted.

The present seems to be a convenient place for some allusion to the subject of compensation for improve-ments. Section 6 of the Act enables a Council to reward a *purchaser* for anything which " increases the value of the holding," while the proviso to *sec.* 4 (2) deals with improvements made by a *tenant*. By this proviso a tenant may remove any fruit or other trees and bushes planted by him, and any shed, &c., built or acquired by him, " for which he has no claim for compensation." The statutes applicable to the case are the Agricultural Holdings Act, 1883, and the Allotments (Compensa-tion for Crops) Act, 1887. The latter Act applies only to parcels of land of two acres, or less, in area.

One most important question will be—Did the tenant obtain the consent in writing of his landlord before making the improvement ? If nay, the question of compensation will often be at an end ; and the tenant will have to consider whether he will remove the thing which constitutes the improvement.

Improvements under the Act of 1883, for which the landlord's consent is not necessary to entitle the tenant

Compensa-
tion for
improve-
ments.

to compensation are : boning with undissolved bones, chalking, claying, liming, marling, and manuring (except, as a rule, during last year of tenancy). Improvements requiring consent are such as these : buildings, silos, permanent pasture, gardens, roads, bridges, watercourses, wells, water supply, fences, orchards, fruit bushes, reclamation of waste lands, embanking, draining, &c.

The Act of 1887 confers on the tenant a right of compensation as to—(1) crops and fruit, fruit trees and bushes planted with landlord's consent; (2) labour expended and manure laid since taking of last crop ; (3) drains, and any outbuildings raised with the landlord's consent.

Purchase-
money.

The purchase-money (which is to include the cost of conveyance incurred by the Council) will be payable

Part
payable on
completion.

thus : On completion of the purchase (not less than a month after the date of purchase) one-fifth of the purchase-money is to be paid in cash; a portion equal to one-fourth, or less, may be secured by a

Rent-
charge.

perpetual rent-charge, which shall be redeemable as provided by the Conveyancing Act, 1881 ; while the

Balance.

balance, not exceeding eleven-twentieths of the purchase-money, will be secured by a charge on the holding repayable by half-yearly instalments within a term of not more than fifty years, or, at the option of the purchaser, by a terminable annuity payable by equal half-yearly instalments. The purchaser may at any time pay off the charge or redeem the annuity.

Perpetual
quit-rent.

The subject of a perpetual rent-charge was debated at great length in the House of Commons. The adoption of a perpetual quit-rent has throughout been strongly advocated by Mr. Jesse Collings as being necessary to enable the purchaser of a holding to keep the maximum portion of his capital available for the purposes of cultivation and improvement, while, at the same time, such a provision tended to prevent the interposition of money-lenders. The main purpose of the Act is the creation of a race of cultivating owners, not a class of small impecunious landlords. It was, however, at length decided to make the rent-charge above mentioned redeemable, while, at the same time, a clause was added conferring a right of pre-emption upon the County Council.

A County Council may agree to postpone for any term not exceeding five years the time for payment of an instalment, or part thereof, either of principal or interest, or of a terminable annuity, in consideration of outlay, made by the purchaser upon his holding, which the Council deem to be an addition to the value of the holding; but this must be done on terms calculated to save the Council from any loss: *sec.* 6. Extension of time for payment.

Each County Council is to keep a register of owners and occupiers of small holdings sold or let, together with a map showing the size, boundaries, and situation of each holding. The County Council must, further-more, cause the purchaser of each holding to be registered under the Land Transfer Act, 1875, as absolute owner thereof; and the provisions of and rules under that Act may be made applicable to small holdings. Subsequent dealings with the land will be greatly facilitated by this registration. If a Council Register of holdings. Land Transfer Act.

Registration of title.

cannot obtain registration with an absolute title, registration with a "qualified title" under the Act of 1875 and the new Rules may be effected.

Conditions of tenure.

Every holding sold by a Council is, for twenty years from the date of the sale, or so long thereafter as any purchase-money remains unpaid, to be held under these conditions—that is to say : (1) that all periodical payments, if any, are duly made ; (2) that the holding is tilled by the purchaser, and used only for agriculture (holdings may be either arable or pastoral) ; (3) that the yeoman does not underlet or subdivide the holding without the consent of the Council ; (4) that only one dwelling-house is erected on a holding, and every such dwelling-house must (5) comply with the requirements of the Council as to sanitation and accommodation for the occupants ; (6) that no house or building on a holding is used for the sale of intoxicating liquors. Moreover, a Council may direct that no building is to be erected on any particular holding without their consent : *sec.* 9.

Penalty for breach of conditions.

The penalty for breach of any of the above-mentioned conditions is that the Council, after calling upon the holder to conform or make reparation, may sell the holding.

Sale after death of holder.

If, owing to the death of the purchaser, a holding, by reason of any devise, bequest, intestacy, or other form of devolution, is liable to become subdivided, the Council may require the holding to be sold, within one year from the decease of the holder, to some one person. If default be made in so selling, the Council may cause the holding to be sold.

While the Small Holdings Bill was passing through Devolution of holding. Committee of the House of Commons a clause was proposed by Mr. Cust providing that the land forming a holding should be deemed to be personalty of the holder, and should be treated as if it were his leasehold ; but succession duty, and not probate or legacy duty, was to be payable in respect of any such holding. This suggested provision was the subject of much discussion. It was felt that it would be unwise to introduce so important a change in the law in what may be called an incidental manner; and the principle of the clause was deemed objectionable by many. It was therefore ultimately struck out of the Bill. The clause, if passed, would have had a beneficial operation in those cases where holders of land had failed, through neglect or ignorance, to make a will effectually disposing of their freeholds. It is hoped, however, that the spread of education will tend to lessen the number of intestacies and defective wills. If the owner of a small holding hereafter die intestate, his land will descend to his heir-at-law, and although there may, in some cases, be difficulty in establishing who he is, the County Council will not often be under the necessity of requiring a sale of the holding to some one person, as in the case with which *sec.* 9 (3) deals.

Any sale made upon such default as last aforesaid, Sale after death of holder or upon breach of condition. or for breach of any of the conditions above mentioned, may be made either subject to the charge on account of purchase-money, or free, wholly or partly, from that charge ; but, in any case, the provisions of the

Sale after death of holder or upon breach of condition.

Act as to purchase-money are to apply as if the sale were a first sale of a holding. The proceeds of sale are to be applied in discharge of any unpaid purchase-money for the holding, or in redemption of any rent-charge or terminable annuity which is not to continue as a charge upon the holding. Any balance will be payable to the person "appearing to the Council to be entitled to receive the same : " *sec.* 9.

Foregoing provisions apply to tenants of small holdings.

When a holding has been let by a Council, the foregoing provisions, except of course those as to purchase-money, are to apply; and upon breach of any term or condition the Council may, after calling upon the tenant to make amends, if such be possible, put an end to the tenancy : *sec.* 9.

Right of pre-emption by County Council.

If the owner of a holding wish to sell or use a holding for purposes other than agriculture, and the restrictive conditions imposed by the Act no longer attach to the holding, he must offer his holding for sale first of all to the County Council; next to the person or persons, if any, entitled to the lands from which the holding was originally severed ; and then to the adjacent owner or owners. Any such holding is to be treated as superfluous land within *secs.* 127–130 of the Lands Clauses Consolidation Act, 1845. The adoption of a provision giving the County Council the right of pre-emption was strongly advocated by Mr. Collings and others, as being necessary for the purpose of preventing any misapplication of the provisions of the Act and the interposition of mortgagees and "money-lenders " generally.

With regard to the Council's right of pre-emption,

it is to be observed that the Select Committee of the House of Commons recommended, in its report dated June, 1890, that power should be given to the County Council to resume possession of small holdings when good use could be made of them for some public object.

The report says:—"Your Committee also recom-
" mend the adoption of the provisions of the Small
" Holdings Bill (Mr. Collings'), by which the local
" authority is empowered to resume possession of the
" property for public purposes, or for building land,
" on payment of full compensation based on its value
" *as an agricultural occupation.* This right must be
" reserved to prevent the use of the land from being
" restricted to agricultural purposes where it may be
" required for the extension of towns and villages,
" and by this means what is called the 'unearned
" increment' will be divided between the occupier
" and the community—that is to say, that any
" increase in value arising from improved communi-
" cation or enhanced price of produce will go to
" the occupier, while the benefit of any change which
" would convert agricultural into town land, and
" which is wholly due to the extension of the popula-
" tion, would go to the district in which such an
" extension had taken place."

It will be interesting to observe whether the creation of this right of re-purchase by the local authority will tend to discourage transactions under the Act; but the Committee felt justified in making the foregoing recommendation on the ground that it was proposed to " offer unexampled facilities to one class of the com-

Right of purchase, if land diverted from agriculture.

" munity," and it was therefore desirable to impose a condition which would protect the rest of the population.

There is an important difference between the proposals of the Committee (adopted from Mr. Collings' Bill) and the provisions of the Act. The recommendation of the Committee was that the local authority should have power to buy for any public object at the price of the land, together with the value of any permanent improvements made by the holder; and Mr. Collings further proposed to give him ten per cent. as compensation for disturbance. Thus, if A. B. had purchased a holding for £500, and his improvements were found to be worth £200, and from some cause, not due to anything done by the holder, his land had become worth £2,000 for (say) building purposes, the local authority would, on the plan suggested, have been able to buy back at (£500 + £200=) £700.

The Small Holdings Act, however, does not restrict the price, and the local authority would, therefore, have to pay the small holder the market price,—that is to say, in the above case, £2,000.

Further reasons for the adoption of a power of preemption were these :—First, it was thought that a landlord would not sell a part of his land for small holdings if it seemed likely that, in the near future (20 years after sale) the land might fall into the hands of some manufacturer or speculative builder, who might do something injurious to the general estate ; and, again, if it were known that the land might, 20 years hence, be quite free from any condition and available for any purpose, then speculators might purchase holdings through the medium of some cultivator, who would work the holding until the 20 years had expired, and then hand over the land to the real purchaser. It was thought that the best way to prevent this prospective speculation and other risks was to confer a right of pre-emption upon the County Council, who, as a representative body, are presumed to do what is best for the locality, and, upon their failing to buy back, then the original vendor or his representative should enjoy a like right, so as to protect the general estate from possible injury.

The Small Holdings Act specially empowers persons Powers of tenants for having the powers of a tenant for life within the life to grant land for meaning of the Settled Land Acts to sell, lease, or holdings. exchange any settled land to or with a County Council; and any such tenant for life may grant the settled land to a Council in perpetuity at a fee-farm or other rent secured by condition of re-entry or otherwise : *secs.* 12, 13.

Whenever any right of grazing, sheepwalk, or other Grazing and other like right is attached to land acquired by a Council rights. for small holdings, the Council may attach *a share* of the right to any such grazing, &c., to any small holding : *sec.* 14.

With regard to the regulation of small holdings Delegation of certain which have no dwelling-houses upon them, a County powers. Council may delegate the business of adaptation of the land for holdings, and the sale, letting, and management of the holdings, to a Committee consisting of the county councillor representing the electoral division in which the holdings are situate; two other members of the Council; two of the allotment

Managing
committee. managers (if any) under the Allotments Act, 1887, for
the parish or area in which the holdings are situate,
selected by those managers, or, if there be no allotment managers, then two persons appointed as provided by the Act of 1887. If, however, the holdings
be situate within the boundary of a municipal borough,
two members of the Town Council take the place of the
two persons last mentioned : *sec.* 16.

*Sitting
tenants.*
Act
extended to
purchasers
of small
holdings
from *private*
landlords.
The special attention of the reader is called to the
section which constitutes Part II. of the Act. That section empowers the Council of any county where a small
holding, or part of one, is situate, to lend to the tenant
of such a holding (upon the security of the same),
when that tenant has agreed to purchase the holding
of his landlord, a sum not exceeding four-fifths of the
purchase-money. This, however, can only be done
when the Council are satisfied that the title is a good
one, and that the sale is made in good faith and at
a reasonable price. These conditions being satisfied,
the provisions of the Act as to purchase-money
become applicable. The reader will readily call to
mind the provisions of the Acts relating to Ireland,
whereby, under conditions, public money may be
Sitting
tenants.
advanced to a tenant for the purchase of his landlord's
interest.

It is hoped that the effect of this important clause
may be to add greatly to the number of cultivating
owners in the country.

Concluding
remarks.
It now only remains to observe that the Act comes
into force on the 1st of October, 1892, and that its
provisions may be put into operation by any County
Council in England, Wales, or Scotland.

SMALL HOLDINGS ACT, 1892.

[55 & 56 Vict. Ch. 31.]

—

ARRANGEMENT OF SECTIONS.

PART I.

3

PART II.

LOANS BY COUNTY COUNCILS TO TENANTS PURCHASING SMALL HOLDINGS.

PART III.

SUPPLEMENTAL.

SMALL HOLDINGS ACT, 1892.

55 & 56 Vict. Chapter 31.

An Act to facilitate the acquisition of Small Agricultural Holdings.   [*27th June*, 1892.]

BE it enacted by the Queen's most Excellent Majesty, by and with the advice and consent of the Lords Spiritual and Temporal, and Commons, in this present Parliament assembled, and by the authority of the same, as follows :—

PART I.

Provision of Small Holdings by County Councils.

1.—(1) If the Council of any county are of opinion that there is such a demand for small holdings in their county as justifies them in putting into operation this part of this Act (*a*), the Council may (*b*), subject to the provisions of this Act, acquire any suitable (*c*) land (*d*) for the purpose of providing small holdings for persons who desire to buy and will themselves cultivate the holdings (*e*).

Power for County Council to acquire land for small holdings.

Sec. 1.

Power for County Council to acquire land for small holdings.

(2) The expression " small holding " for the purposes of this Act shall mean land acquired by a Council under the powers and for the purposes of this Act, and which exceeds one acre (*f*), and either does not exceed fifty acres, or, if exceeding fifty acres, is of an annual value for the purposes of the income tax not exceeding fifty pounds (*g*).

(*a*) This subsection must be read in conjunction with the whole of section 5, which directs what steps shall be taken for the purpose of deciding whether it is expedient to put the Act into force. The first subsec. of sec. 5 places the duty of taking the initiative chiefly upon the County Council itself. This being so, and due regard being had to the provisions of subsec. 2 of sec. 5, the County Council will do well to overlook any defects of form and expression in any petition presented by county electors or a county elector.

The words " for the labouring population " after the words " in their county " were struck out of the Bill, when in Committee of the House of Commons, so as to leave the Act without restriction as to the classes from which purchasers and hirers of small holdings might come.

(*b*) This was specially so worded (" may "), notwithstanding many objections made in the House of Commons, so as to give entire and unfettered discretion to the County Councils with respect to the adoption of the Act.

(*c*) That is to say, " suitable " so far as the Council are able, with the local knowledge at command, to judge.

(*d*) By sec. 20 the term " land " includes " any right or easement in or over land," *i.e.*, any existing right whatsoever which is essential to the due adaptation of the land acquired for small holdings. *See* sec. 18 as to the *restrictions* upon the power of a Council to acquire land for the purposes of the Act.

The Act imposes no restriction as to the *place* where the land proposed to be used for small holdings is to be situate. The

Council of a county-borough may, therefore, acquire land for small holdings outside the municipal boundary. But other County Councils will, no doubt, mostly find it possible and expedient to get land within their own county.

(e) There are thus two conditions precedent, that is to say, persons must (1) desire to buy, and must (2) undertake to themselves cultivate the land. The Act, however, provides for some special cases where a County Council may *hire* (on lease or otherwise) and *let*. *See* secs. 2 and 4 (2), *post*. The proposed purchasers of small holdings must be fit persons ; and the Council have very wide and full powers, under sec. 7, to make rules for " guarding against any small holding being let or sold to any person who is unable to cultivate it properly, and otherwise for securing the proper cultivation of a holding." *See* sec. 7 (c). It was at first intended to require a third condition, viz., that persons proposing to purchase small holdings should be resident within the county, but this provision was, as the result of debate, struck out of the Bill.

As to the mode of acquisition of land by a Council, *see* sec. 3, *post*.

By the Interpretation Act, 1889, sec. 1 (1), in every Act passed after the year 1850, unless the contrary appears, words importing the masculine gender include females. Hence a woman may purchase or hire a small holding from a County Council.

(f) If it did not exceed one acre, a holding would belong to the rank of allotments. The Allotments Acts, however, contain no definition of the term *allotment ;* but it seems to follow from the language of the Act of 1887 that one person is not to have an allotment of more than one acre in area, and that an allotment is a parcel of land held by a tenant and intended to be cultivated by a person belonging to the labouring population : *vide* 50 & 51 Vict. c. 48, secs. 6 (1) and 7 (6).

Sec. 17 of the same Act says that " the expression ' allotment ' includes a field-garden." This last term is employed in the General Enclosure Acts to express what is now known as an allotment, and in those Acts it meant the whole piece of land appropriated by the valuer for the labouring poor, or for any other

Sec. 1.

Power for County Council to acquire land for small holdings.

Sec. 1.

Power for
County
Council to
acquire
land for
small
holdings.

public purpose, or to a private owner. *See*, further, Mr. T. HALL HALL's work on the Allotments Act.

The Small Holdings Act deals specially with the subject of *ownership*, while the Allotments Acts relate wholly to *tenancies*.

(*g*) One curious result follows—or, rather, may follow—from the construction of this subsection, viz., that a small holding may be of less area than fifty acres, but, at the same time, it may be of greater "annual value for the purposes of the income tax" than £50.

County
Council
may lease
land in lieu
of pur-
chasing.

2.—Where land, through its proximity to a town or suitability for building purposes, or for any other special reason, has a prospective value which in the opinion of the County Council is too high to make its purchase for agricultural purposes desirable, the Council may hire the land on lease or otherwise for the purpose of letting it in small holdings in accordance with the provisions of this Act (*a*).

(*a*) *Cf.* sec. 4 (2), *post*. The provisions of sec. 2 are intended to be put into operation only when it is quite clear that a *purchase* of the land could not be effected at a price which would enable the Council to sell or let otherwise than at a loss. The object of the Act is to establish, if possible, a class of *cultivating owners*, and the Council is to assume the character of landlord (a position which a public body fills with much difficulty) only in the special cases for which sec. 2 and sec. 4 (2) provide.

Purchase of
land and
adaptation
of it for
small
holdings.

3.—(1) For the purpose of the purchase of land under this Act by a County Council the Lands Clauses Acts shall be incorporated with this Act, except the provisions of those Acts with respect to the purchase and taking of land otherwise than by agreement, which provisions shall not apply for the purposes of this Act (*a*) ; and section one hundred and

38 & 39 Vict.
c. 55.

seventy-eight of the Public Health Act, 1875 (*b*),

shall apply as if the County Council were referred to therein.

Sec. 3.

Purchase cf
land and
adaptation
of it for
small
holdings.

(2) The County Council may, if they think fit, before sale or letting, adapt for small holdings any land acquired under this Act by dividing and fencing it, making occupation roads, and executing any other works, such as works for the provision of drainage or water supply, which can in the opinion of the Council be more economically and efficiently executed for the land as a whole (c).

(3) The County Council may also, if they think fit, as part of the agreement for the sale or letting of a small holding, adapt the land for a small holding by erecting thereon such buildings, or making such adaptations of existing buildings, as in their opinion are required for the due occupation of the holding, and cannot be made by the purchaser or tenant (d).

(a) The following appear to be the sections of the Lands Clauses Act, 1845, incorporated by this section :—

Sections 6 to 15 (both inclusive) : *Purchase of lands by agreement.*

„   69 to 83 „   „   *Application of purchase-money and compensation.*

„   84 to 92 „   „   *Entry upon lands purchased.*

„   93 and 94 : *Intersected lands.*

„   95 to 98 (both inclusive): *Copyhold lands.*

„   99 to 107 „   „   *Common and waste lands.*

„   108 to 114 „   „   *Lands under mortgage.*

„   115 to 118 „   „   *Rent-charges, chief and other rents.*

„   119 to 123 „   „   *Leases.*

Sec. 3.

Purchase of
land and
adaptation
of it for
small
holdings.

Sections 124 to 126 (both inclusive): *Interests omitted to be purchased.*

,,   128 to 132 ,,   ,,   *Sale of superfluous lands.*
(*See* sec. 15 of the Small Holdings Act.)

,,   136 to 145 (both inclusive): *Recovery of penalties.*

,,   146 to 149 .,   ,,   *Appeal.*

The Act of 1845 has been amended by the following Acts :
45 & 46 Vict. c. 38, sec. 32 ; 45 & 46 Vict. c. 15. Sec. 10 of 8
& 9 Vict. c. 18 was extended by 23 & 24 Vict. c. 106, sec. 2.

(*b*) This sec. empowers the Chancellor and Council of the
Duchy of Lancaster to sell lands belonging to the Duchy.

(*c*) The Council will put the provisions of this subsec. into
operation only when the circumstances of the case render it
probable in their opinion that such works as fencing, road-
making, and draining can be carried out at a smaller outlay by
the Council than they could be by the purchasers or tenants.
It will be noticed that these works are to be executed *before*
steps have been taken to sell or let.

(*d*) The power to raise buildings relates, of course, to each
individual holding, and will be properly exercised when it has
been found that the particular purchaser or tenant is unable
to erect or adapt the buildings required.

4.—(1) The County Council shall apportion the
total cost of the acquisition of the land, and of any
adaptation thereof, among the several holdings in
such manner as seems just (*a*), and shall, save as
hereinafter mentioned (*b*), offer the small holdings
for sale in accordance with rules under this Act (*c*).

(2) Where the County Council are of opinion that
any persons desirous of themselves cultivating small
holdings are unable to buy, on the terms fixed by this
Act, or where the land has been hired by the Council
on lease or otherwise, the Council may, in the case of
any small holding which either does not exceed fifteen

acres in extent, or, if exceeding fifteen acres, is of the Sec. 4.
annual value for the purpose of the income tax not Sale or letting of small holdings.
exceeding fifteen pounds (*d*), instead of offering it for
sale, offer to let it in accordance with rules under this
Act (*e*).

Provided that a tenant of any small holding may,
before the expiration of his tenancy, remove any fruit
and other trees and bushes planted or acquired by him
for which he has no claim for compensation, and
remove any toolhouse, shed, greenhouse, fowlhouse, or
pigsty built or acquired by him for which he has no
claim for compensation (*f*).

(3) The County Council shall have power to sell,
or, in the case of small holdings which may be let, to
let one or more small holdings to a number of persons
working on a co-operative system, provided such
system be approved by the County Council (*g*).

(4) The cost of acquisition and adaptation shall for
the purposes of this section include every expense
incurred by the Council in relation to the land,
inclusive of any allowance to any officers of the
Council for work done in relation thereto.

(*a*) The Council therefore has an absolute discretion (as the
varying circumstances of each place require) as to how the
total cost of acquisition and adaptation is to be apportioned
among the holdings.

(*b*) *See* secs. 6 and 7, *post.*

(*c*) When the Council have caused the land acquired to be cut
up into holdings of the sizes which circumstances seem to
demand, the next step will be to determine what rights of way

and other easements (if any) should be attached to each holding ;
and to apportion the rights (if any) of grazing, sheepwalk and
other such rights.   This being done, a further question will be
the making of fences, occupation roads, drains and the like, in
short, all works which, in the opinion of the Council, can " be
more economically and efficiently executed for the land as a
whole : " sec. 3 (2), *ante*. Yet another matter, after the land has
been prepared *as a whole*, will be the provision of new, or
adaptation of existing, buildings for each holding : sec. 3 (3),
ante.

(*d*) It might happen that a holding, although less than
15 acres in area, is of greater yearly value for purposes of
income tax than £15.

(*e*)   Compare sec. 2, *ante*.
There is nothing in this clause which entitles a Council to
impose any kind of undertaking upon the hirer of land that he
will, in the future, become a purchaser, although the Act is
essentially an Act for the creation of ownerships, and it is hoped
that many who hire at first will afterwards be able to purchase.
The Council may let either purchased or hired land : sec. 4 (2).

(*f*) Compensation may be allowable by custom, or under the
Agricultural Holdings Act, 1883, or the Allotments Compensation for Crops Act, 1887.   The first point to be considered under
the above proviso is as to the law applicable to the case.   The
Act of 1883 relates to every " parcel of land held by a tenant,"
whatever its area, if only the holding be "either wholly agricultural or wholly pastoral or in part agricultural, and as to the
residue pastoral, or in whole or in part cultivated as a market
garden : " 46 & 47 Vict. c. 61, sec. 54.   The Act of 1887
relates to any "parcel of land, of not more than two acres in
extent, held by a tenant under a landlord and cultivated as a
garden or as a farm, or partly as a garden and partly as a farm."
Hence there may be holdings which do not come under the definition in either Act, while in other cases both Acts may be
applicable.

The things for which compensation is made by custom are

of four classes : (1) Permanent improvements (*e.g.*, drainage) ;   Sec. 4.
(2) Durable improvements (*e.g.*, liming) ; (3) Temporary   Sale or
improvements (*e.g.*, manuring) ; (4) Acts of continuing cultiva- letting of
tion (*e.g.*, labour, seed).   small
holdings.

The improvements to which the Act of 1883 applies are : (1)
Buildings, silos, pasture, irrigation works, gardens, roads, bridges,
fencing, fruit planting, embanking. (2) Drainage. To both
these classes the written consent of the landlord must be first had
to entitle to compensation. (3) Boning, chalking, clay burning,
use of artificial manure ; consumption by cattle, sheep and pigs
of food stuffs not produced on the holding. Here only notice
of claim to compensation need be given to the landlord. *See*
JEUDWINE on the Agricultural Holdings Act, 1883.

The things for which compensation is payable under the Act
of 1887 are : (1) Crops, including fruit, growing upon a holding
in the ordinary course of cultivation, fruit trees and bushes
planted with landlord's consent ; (2) Labour and manure used
since taking of last crop and in anticipation of a future crop ;
(3) Drains, outbuildings, &c., constructed with landlord's consent. *Vide* 50 & 51 Vict. c. 26, sec. 5.

It is probable that a tenant will have the right of removal in
most cases where, the landlord's consent not having been
obtained, the question of compensation does not arise. Moreover,
a tenant will not always be entitled to compensation for things
planted.

The expression " other trees " in the proviso to sec. 4 (2) of
the Small Holdings Act might be held to mean trees *ejusdem
generis*, and would therefore not include timber trees. If it
were so decided by the Court, the outgoing tenant would seem
to have no right of removal.

See sec. 9 (7) as to the conditions under which a small holding
let by a Council is to be held.

(g) This is, in the opinion of many, one of the most important
and valuable provisions in the whole Act, for it will enable persons to unite their forces for the common benefit. *See* p. 9,
ante. The effect of the clause is that where two or more men
desire and agree to work together on the co-operative principle,

—that is to say, doing the work of cultivation themselves and sharing the profits—the County Council may sell to them more than one small holding. Thus, two or more men in a village may put their capital together, form themselves into a co-operative society, and purchase under this Act 20 or 50 acres, or whatever their means will allow, and then proceed to work their holdings under rules which have been approved by the County Council.

5.—(1) Any County Council may, and every County Council not being a Council of a county borough shall (*a*), appoint a committee (*b*) to consider whether the circumstances of the county justify the Council in putting into operation this part of this Act.

(2) Any one or more county electors may present a petition to the Council of their county alleging that there is a demand for small holdings in the county, and praying that this part of this Act may be put in operation (*c*), and thereupon the petition shall be referred to the committee appointed under this section, who, on being satisfied that the petition is presented in good faith and on reasonable grounds, shall forthwith cause an inquiry (*d*) into the circumstances to be made, and shall report the result to the Council (*c*).

(3) If any councillor representing or alderman residing in any electoral division of a county in which it is alleged that there is a demand for small holdings is not a member of the committee, he shall be added to the committee for the consideration of the alleged demand.

(*a*) That is to say, it is entirely in the discretion of the Council of a county-borough whether or not a committee shall be appointed, under this section, to consider whether it is expedient to put the Act into operation. On the other hand, every Council of a county (using the word in the popular sense) is bound to appoint such a committee. This section must be read together with section 1.

(*b*) It is clearly the intention of the framers of the Act that the duties of the Council under the Act shall be performed chiefly by means of a committee. Subsec. 3 of this section makes it obvious that the committee should be thoroughly representative ; and County Councils will, no doubt, select the best practical men that are available. The practical working of the Act, when adopted, may be delegated to another committee, which also is to be thoroughly representative. *See* sec. 16, *post*. Moreover, by sec. 7 a Council has power to make rules for carrying the Act into effect, save as otherwise provided in the Act—that is to say, the local authority enjoys entire freedom of action on all points for which the Act makes no specific provision.

(*c*) The whole initiative is, therefore, not left in the hands of the Council, for by this clause a county elector or (in a county-borough) a burgess may make representations, which may be in the ordinary form of a petition, to the Council. *See* Appendix B, *post*.

(*d*) The Council has complete freedom and discretion as to how this inquiry is to be conducted. It is most likely that it will be found convenient to delegate the duty of holding the inquiry to some member or members of the committee or other responsible persons who possess local knowledge.

(*e*) The Council will then express its will in the matter by resolution. *See* sec. 1, subsec. 1.

6.—(1) The purchase-money for each small holding sold by the County Council shall include the costs of registration of title (*a*), but shall not include any expense incurred by the purchaser for legal or other advice or assistance,

(2) Every purchaser shall, within such time, not

Sec. 6.

Regulations
as to pur-
chase-
money and
sale. less than one month after the purchase, as is fixed by rules under this Act (*b*), complete the purchase.

(3) On such completion he shall pay not less than one-fifth of the purchase-money.

(4) A portion representing not more than one-fourth of the purchase-money may, if the County Council think fit, be secured by a perpetual rent-charge, which shall be redeemable in manner directed by section forty-five of the Conveyancing and Law of 44 & 45 Vict.
c. 41. Property Act, 1881, with respect to rent-charges to which that section applies (*c*).

(5) The residue (if any) of the purchase-money shall be secured by a charge on the holding in favour of the Council, and shall either be repaid by half-yearly instalments of principal with such interest, and within such term, not exceeding fifty years from the date of the sale, as may be agreed on with the Council, or shall, if the purchaser so requires, be repaid with such interest and within such term as aforesaid by a terminable annuity payable by equal half-yearly instalments. The amount for the time being unpaid may at any time be discharged, and any such terminable annuity may at any time be redeemed, in accordance with tables fixed by the County Council (*d*).

(6) The Council may, if they think fit, agree to postpone for a term not exceeding five years the time for payment of all or any part of an instalment either of principal or interest, or of a terminable annuity, in consideration of expenditure by the purchaser which, in the opinion of the Council, increases the value of

the holding, but shall do so on such terms as will, in their opinion, prevent them from incurring any loss (*e*).

(7) A small holding may be sold subject to such rights of way or other rights for the benefit of other small holdings as the Council consider necessary or expedient.

Sec. 6.

Regulations as to purchase-money and sale.

(*a*) *See* section 10 (1), *post.*

(*b*) No rules as to this have yet been issued.

(*c*) Section 45 of the Conveyancing and Law of Property Act, 1881, is as follows :—

" (1) Where there is a quit-rent, chief-rent, rent-charge, or " other annual sum issuing out of land (in this section referred " to as the rent), the Copyhold Commissioners [now the Board " of Agriculture, 52 & 53 Vict. c. 30, s. 2 (1) *b*] shall, at any " time, on the requisition of the owner of the land, or of any " person interested therein, certify the amount of money in " consideration whereof the rent may be redeemed.

" (2) Where the person entitled to the rent is absolutely " entitled thereto in fee simple in possession, or is empowered " to dispose thereof absolutely, or to give an absolute discharge " for the capital value thereof, the owner of the land, or any " person interested therein, may, after serving one month's " notice on the person entitled to the rent, pay or tender to " that person the amount certified by the Commissioners."

NOTE TO SUBSEC. 2.—It is understood that the Board do not act under this subsection in cases where there is a trust for, or power of, sale of the rent. Clearly the subsection applies to cases where there is a trust for sale. The trustees are empowered "to dispose thereof absolutely," and also to give "an absolute discharge for the capital value," and are also the persons entitled to the rent, and consequently the persons to whom notice is to be given and tender made. Where there is a power of sale in trustees of a settlement or in the tenant for life under the Settled Land Acts, it is conceived that the tenant for life and the trustees together

Sec. 6.

Regulations
as to pur-
chase-
money and
sale.

are the persons "empowered to dispose thereof absolutely," and are the persons entitled to the rent and to whom notice is to be given. WOLSTENHOLME and BRINTON on the *Conveyancing and Settled Land Acts*, 6th ed., p. 106.

" (3) On proof to the Commissioners that payment or tender
" has been so made, they shall certify that the rent is redeemed
" under this Act ; and that certificate shall be final and con-
" clusive, and the land shall be thereby absolutely freed and
" discharged from the rent.

" (4) Every requisition under this section shall be in
" writing ; and every certificate under this section shall be in
" writing sealed with the seal of the Commissioners.

" (5) This section does not apply to tithe rent-charge or to
" a rent reserved on a sale or lease, or to a rent made payable
" under a grant or licence for building purposes, or to any
" sum or payment issuing out of land not being perpetual.

" (6) This section applies to rents payable at, or created
" after, the commencement of this Act.

" (7) This section does not extend to Ireland."

NOTE.—The entire expense of redeeming the rent necessarily falls on the person redeeming. He has to procure the certificate of the Board as to the amount to be paid, and as to payment or tender of that amount. The person entitled to the rent has only to receive the redemption money. WOLSTENHOLME and BRINTON, *Conveyancing Acts*, 6th ed., p. 107.

As to obtaining apportionment of rents mentioned in this section, *see* 17 & 18 Vict. c. 97, secs. 10–14.

The Act says nothing as to how the perpetual rent-charge by which one-fourth of the purchase-money may be secured is to be calculated, and it is also silent as to the rate of interest on the residue (*see* next subsec.).

(*d*) When payment is by instalments of principal and interest, the amount payable is, of course, less at every successive payment. The *amount* of the instalment is the same on each occasion, but the interest obviously less, for the total is smaller. When, however, payment is by a terminable annuity, the amount payable each half-year is the same throughout the period.

Suppose the purchase-money to be £500. The purchaser must
pay £100 on completion ; and if the portion secured by rent-
charge be the maximum, viz., £125, the balance will be £275.
Then, assuming that the rate of interest agreed on be 4 per
cent. and the term of repayment 50 years, the purchaser would, if
the residue were £275, pay, under the first of the two alternative
modes of repayment, £2 15s. capital and £5 10s. interest at the
end of the first half-year, and £5 8s. 11d. interest at the end of
the second half-year, and so on throughout the whole period
of 50 years, the interest being gradually reduced ; while, under
the second of the two alternative modes of repayment, he would
pay at the end of each half-year throughout the whole period of
50 years, on the basis of Archer's tables, the sum of £6 7s. 7¼d.

(e) The Act, instead of authorising a loan to a purchaser of a
holding who has made outlay which increases the value of the
holding, enables the Council to postpone the time for payment
of principal or interest, as herein enacted. Nice questions are
likely to arise as to what is an increase of value ; but, beyond a
doubt, this clause is intended to benefit those who have executed
improvements of a more or less permanent and lasting nature,
e.g., drainage, water supply, dealings with waste land, buildings,
planting of fruit and other trees, &c.

7.—Every County Council acquiring land (*a*) under
this Act shall make rules for carrying into effect this
Act, except as otherwise provided, and in particular—

(*a*) as to the manner in which holdings are to be
sold or let, or offered for sale or letting ; and

(*b*) as to notice to be given of the offer for sale or
letting ; and

(*c*) for guarding against any small holding being
let or sold to a person who is unable to cultivate
it properly, and otherwise for securing the proper
cultivation of a holding (*b*).

(*a*) *See* the definition of the term " land " in sec. 20.

4

Sec. 7.

Rules as to mode and conditions of sale.

(*b*) This section, as the reader will see at once, confers upon the County Council very wide powers for the making of all regulations necessary to ensure the efficient working of the Act. The insertion of a clause like the above was inevitable, having regard to the fact that no legislative measure can make effective provision for cases which are wholly the result of local circumstances. Hence it is that, while the Act tells us how, and within what bounds, a County Council may acquire land for small holdings, it has to leave the Council an absolute discretion as to the details of working, and especially, as the above section says, with regard to the mode of sale and letting and the conditions to be imposed for the purpose of securing that holdings are sold or let only to fit persons, who will cultivate them in a manner which can be considered good husbandry. So entire is the freedom of action that it is necessary to repose in the local authority, that by sec. 9 (6) a County Council may, under special circumstances, sell, or allow to be sold, a holding free from any, or all, of the conditions imposed by sec. 9.

List to be kept by County Council.

8.—Every County Council shall keep a list of the owners and occupiers of small holdings sold or let by them, and a map or plan showing the size, boundaries, and situation of each small holding so sold or let.

Conditions affecting small holdings.

9.—(1) Every small holding sold by a County Council under this Act shall for a term of twenty years (*a*) from the date of the sale, and thereafter so long as any part of the purchase-money remains unpaid, be held subject to the following conditions :—

(*a*) That any periodical payments due in respect of the purchase-money shall be duly made ;

(*b*) That the holding shall not be divided, subdivided, assigned, let or sublet without the consent of the County Council (*b*) ;

(*c*) That the holding shall be cultivated by the

owner or occupier as the case may be, and shall not be used for any purpose other than agriculture (c) ;

(d) That not more than one dwelling-house shall be erected on the holding ;

(e) That any dwelling-house erected on the holding shall comply with such requirements as the County Council may impose for securing healthiness and freedom from overcrowding ;

(f) That no dwelling-house or building on the holding shall be used for the sale of intoxicating liquors (d) ;

(g) In the case of any holding on which, in the opinion of the County Council, a dwelling-house ought not to be erected, that no dwelling-house shall be erected on the holding without the consent of the County Council.

(2) If any such condition is broken, the Council may, after giving the owner an opportunity of remedying the breach, if it is capable of remedy, cause the holding to be sold (e).

(3) If on the decease of the owner while the holding is subject to the conditions imposed by this section, the holding would, by reason of any devise (f), bequest, intestacy, or otherwise, become subdivided, the Council may require the holding to be sold within twelve months after such decease to some one person, and if default is made in so selling the holding, the Council may cause the holding to be sold.

(4) Any sale by the County Council under this section may be made either subject to the charge in

Sec. 9.

Conditions affecting small holdings.

respect of purchase-money or free, wholly or partly, from that charge, and in either case the provisions of this Act with respect to the purchase-money (*g*) shall apply in like manner as if the sale were the first sale of a small holding under this Act.

(5) The proceeds of the sale shall be applied in discharge of any unpaid purchase-money for the holding or redemption of any rent-charge or terminable annuity which is not to continue a charge on the holding, and, subject as aforesaid, shall be paid to the person appearing to the Council to be entitled to receive the same.

(6) The County Council may, under special circumstances, to be recorded in their minutes, sell or consent to the sale under this section of a small holding free from all or any of the conditions imposed by this section, and may give such consent on such terms as they think fit (*h*).

(7) Every small holding let by a County Council under the foregoing provisions of this Act shall be held subject to the conditions on which it would under this section be held if it were sold, except so far as those conditions relate to the purchase-money; and if any such condition or any term of the letting is broken the Council may, after giving the tenant an opportunity of remedying the breach (if it is capable of remedy) determine the tenancy (*i*).

(8) Nothing in or done under this section shall derogate from the effect of any building or sanitary byelaws for the time being in force.

(*a*) This term of twenty years was, after much debate in the

House of Commons, agreed upon as being long enough to
prevent any serious misapplication or abuse of the provisions of
the Act. It was thought better to adopt a plan of this kind
rather than impose a condition which would have amounted to a
deduction from the character of freehold as regards the land
sold by the Council.

Vide Nos. 22–24 of the Land Registry Rules, Appendix C, *post.*

(*b*) This condition will have many important effects. First
of all it will ensure the preservation of the holdings in the form
adopted by the Council when the land was cut up. The condition against letting prevents the holding falling into the hands
of an incompetent or unfit person, and the same result follows
(*inter alia*) from the condition against assigning. But a still
more important question is this : What is the effect of the condition against assigning ?   Does it refer only to a transfer from
one person to another of the interest of the cultivating owner, as
such ; or does it amount to a prohibition of any conveyance of
the owner's legal estate, without the consent of the County
Council ?   It would seem that the *former* is the case for which
sec. 9 (1 *b*) is intended to provide ; and therefore it appears to be
open to a cultivating owner to create a mortgage upon his
holding.   But it is probable that some difficulty would be
experienced in borrowing money upon the security of a holding,
for, in the first place, no agreement between an owner and his
mortgagee could over-ride the interests of the County Council in
the holding ; and, moreover, if a mortgagee or other owner of a
charge upon a holding foreclosed or took possession of the holding
under his powers, there would at once be a breach of the conditions imposed by sec. 9. *Vide* Nos. 38 and 39 of the Land
Registry Rules, Appendix C, *post.*   It seems also that a *settlement*
of a holding might be productive of a like result. With regard
to *settlement, see* sec. 49 of the Land Transfer Act, 1875.

The provisions of this sec. (9) suggest a number of questions
fit for judicial interpretation.

(*c*) By sec. 20, "agriculture" and "cultivation" include
" horticulture and the use of land for any purpose of husbandry,

Sec. 9.

Conditions affecting small holdings.

inclusive of the keeping or breeding of any live stock, poultry or bees, and the growth of fruit, vegetables, *and the like.*"

(*d*) This desirable provision was added to the section on the motion of Mr. Joshua Rowntree, late M.P. for Scarborough.

(*e*) *See* subsecs. 4 and 5, which are ancillary to this subsec. The power of sale here conferred ought to effectually prevent any abuse of the provisions of the Act.

(*f*) The purchaser of a holding may, of course, give his holding, by his will, to whomsoever he wishes ; but, if he desire to prevent a sale of the holding by the Council, it will be necessary to devise it to some one person who will be able to comply with the conditions, whatever these may be, imposed by the Council. The devisee of a holding will be registered pursuant to 38 & 39 Vict. c. 87, s. 41.

It is important to note here the provisions of the Intestates Estates Act, 1890. By that Act (53 & 54 Vict. c. 29) the real and personal estates of every man who dies intestate after September 1, 1890, leaving a widow, but no issue, shall, in all cases where the net value of such real and personal estates does not exceed £500, belong to his widow absolutely and exclusively. When the net value of the real and personal estates exceeds £500, the widow is entitled to £500, part thereof, absolutely and exclusively, and has a charge upon the whole property, real and personal, for the £500, with interest at 4 per cent. from the date of death of the intestate. The said charge is to be borne rateably by the real and personal estates ; and the foregoing provisions are without prejudice to the widow's interest in the residue of the realty and personalty.

Vide Nos. 25–30 of the Land Registry Rules, Appendix C, *post.*

(*g*) *See* sec. 6, *ante.*

(*h*) It is clear from the language of this subsection that the wide powers conferred hereby are to be exercised only when some injustice or undesirable result would follow from allowing the condition imposed by the section to take effect. The restrictions imposed by the Act should be relaxed by a County Council with extreme caution.

(*i*) *See* sec. 4, subsec. 2, *ante.*

10.—(1) When a County Council have pur-chased land under this Act, they shall apply for their registration as proprietors thereof with an absolute title under the Land Transfer Act, 1875 (*a*).

(2) Rules under the Land Transfer Act, 1875, (*b*) may—

(*a*) adapt that Act to the registration of small holdings, with such modifications as appear to be required ; and

(*b*) on the application and at the expense of a County Council provide, by the appointment of local agents or otherwise, for carrying into effect the objects of this section.

(*a*) The Rules issued in pursuance of this sec. will be found in Appendix C, *post*.

For a full explanation of the purposes and provisions of the Land Transfer Act the reader is referred to Mr. E. H. HOLT's book on the subject, published in 1876. The main objects of the Act were to shorten the period between agreement for sale and purchase and completion of purchase, and to prevent the repetition of the process of investigation of title. The first registered proprietor, with an absolute title, acquires, forthwith upon registration, an indefeasible title.

Registration under the Act is of three kinds—(1) with an *absolute* title ; (2) with a *possessory* title ; (3) with a *qualified* title. The first of these vests in the person registered as pro-prietor an estate in fee simple in such land, together with all rights, privileges and appurtenances belonging or appurtenant thereto subject—(i.) to the incumbrances (if any) on the register ; (ii.) unless the contrary is expressed on the register, to such liabilities, &c., as are declared by the Act not to be incum-brances (*see* 38 & 39 Vict. c. 87, sec. 18) ; (iii.) when the first registered proprietor is not entitled for his own benefit to the

Sec. 10.

Registration of title to small holdings.

land registered as between himself and any persons claiming under him, to any unregistered estates, rights, interests or equities to which such persons may be entitled ; but free from all other estates and interests of Her Majesty, her heirs and successors. Registration with a *possessory* title is not applicable to the Small Holdings Act. As to the third class, it seems that registration with a qualified title can only be made on *bonâ fide* application for an absolute title ; but the registrar cannot judge of the *bonâ fides* of an applicant, and therefore cannot refuse to entertain an application, however recent may be the beginning of the title. The applicant must show the best title he can, and thereupon registration with a qualified title has the same effect as registration with an absolute title, subject to the excepted estates, rights and interests : 38 & 39 Vict. c. 87, sec. 9. As to registration of title of a *lessor*, *see* 38 & 39 Vict. c. 87, sec. 11.

A County Council may apply to the registrar for the reference of the title to any land purchased, or about to be purchased, to a conveyancing counsel, and the registrar may so refer if he think fit. *See* No. 9 of the new Rules, Appendix C, *post*.

Right of purchase, if land diverted from agriculture.

11.—If at any time after the restrictive conditions (*a*) imposed by this Act have ceased to attach to a small holding, the owner of the holding desires to use the holding for purposes other than agriculture (*b*), he shall before so doing, whether the holding is situate within a town or built upon or not, offer the holding for sale, first to the County Council from whom the holding was purchased (*c*), next to the person or persons (if any) then entitled to the lands from which the holding was originally severed, and then to the person or persons whose lands immediately adjoin the holding, and sections one hundred and twenty-seven to one hundred and thirty of the Lands Clauses Consolidation Act, 1845, shall apply as if the owner of the small holding were the promoter of the under-

8 & 9 Vict. c. 18.

taking, and the holding were superfluous lands within the meaning of those sections (*d*).

Sec. 11.

Right of
purchase
if land
diverted
from agri-
culture.

(*a*) *See*, as to these conditions, sec. 9, *ante.*

(*b*) By sec. 20 of the Act the expression "agriculture" includes horticulture and the use of the land for any purpose of husbandry, inclusive of the keeping or breeding of live stock, poultry or bees, and the growth of fruit, vegetables and the like.

(*c*) *See* p. 18, *ante.* This provision, whereby the County Council will have the right of pre-emption, has been made for the purpose of preventing, as far as possible, any misapplication of the Act, and of discouraging the intervention of mortgagees and money-lenders generally.

(*d*) Compare sec. 15, *post*, p. 28. For the text of secs. 127 to 130 of 8 & 9 Vict. c. 18, and a full explanation of them, *see* WOOLF and MIDDLETON on *Compensation*, p. 243 *et seq.* ; CRIPPS on *Compensation*, chap. xix.

12.—Where a person having the powers of a tenant for life (*a*), within the meaning of the Settled Land Act, 1882, sells, exchanges, or leases any settled land to a County Council for the purposes of this Act, such sale (*b*), exchange (*c*), or lease (*d*) may be made at such a price, or for such consideration, or at such rent as, having regard to the said purposes and to all the circumstances of the case, is the best that can be reasonably obtained (*e*).

(*a*) The expression "tenant for life" is thus defined in sub-sec. 5 of sec. 2 of the Settled Land Act, 1882 : "The person " who is for the time being, under a settlement, beneficially " entitled to possession of settled land for his life, is, for pur-" poses of this Act, the tenant for life of that land and the tenant " for life under that settlement." To this clause the next sub-sec. is ancillary : "(6) If, in any case, there are two or more " persons so entitled as tenants in common, or as joint tenants,

Sec. 12.

Extension of provisions of 45 & 46 Vict. c. 38.

"or for other concurrent estates or interests, they together "constitute the tenant for life for purposes of this Act." *See*, further, WOLSTENHOLME and BRINTON, *Conveyancing and Settled Land Acts*, 6th ed., p. 226 *et seq.*

The class of limited owners is defined in sec. 58 of the Settled Land Act, 1882, *quod vide.* WOLSTENHOLME and BRINTON, p. 309.

(*b*) *Vide* Settled Land Act, 1882 (45 & 46 Vict. c. 38), secs. 2, 3 ; WOLSTENHOLME and BRINTON, pp. 244–248.

(*c*) *Vide* Settled Land Act, 1882, secs. 3, 4 ; WOLSTENHOLME and BRINTON, pp. 247–8.

(*d*) *Ibid.*, secs. 6–14 ; WOLSTENHOLME and BRINTON, pp. 249–259.

(*e*) *Cf.* sec. 4 of Settled Land Act, 1882.

Power to limited owner to sell at a fee-farm rent.

13.—A person having the powers of a tenant for life within the meaning of the Settled Land Act, 1882 (*a*), may grant the settled land, or a part thereof, to a County Council for the purposes of this Act in perpetuity, at a fee-farm (*b*) or other rent (*c*) secured by condition of re-entry, or otherwise as may be agreed upon (*d*).

(*a*) *Vide* sec. 12.

(*b*) This term is thus defined in *Les Termes de la Ley*, A.D. 1641 : "Fee farme is when a tenant holdeth of his Lord in fee "simple paying to him the value of halfe, or of the third part, or "of the fourth part or of the [*i.e.*, any] other part of the land by "the yeere. And hee that holdeth by fee farme ought not to "pay reliefe or do any other thing that is contained in the "feoffement, but fealty, for that belongeth to all kind of "tenures." Mr. GOODEVE says : "The true meaning of 'fee-"farm' seems to be a perpetual farm or rent, the name being "founded on the perpetuity of the rent, not on the *quantum :*" *Real Property*, 3rd ed., p. 348.

(*c*) There are three kinds of rent, viz.—(1) Rent service ;

(2) rent-charge ; (3) rent seck. As to the nature of these and the mode of their creation, *vide* TUDOR's *Leading Cases on* *Real Property*, notes to *Chin's Case ;* GOODEVE, 3rd ed., p. 345 *et seq.* All rents are now recoverable by distress : 4 Geo. II. c. 28, sec. 5.

(*d*) *Vide* No. 3 of the Land Registry Rules, Appendix C, *post.* By the Conveyancing Act, 1881, sec. 44, under instruments coming into operation after 1881, if, and so far as a contrary intention is not expressed thereby, when a person is entitled to receive out of any land, or its income, any annual sum charged on the land or income, by way of rent-charge or otherwise, *not being rent incident to a reversion*, he is to have, so far as they might have been conferred by the instrument, the following remedies, viz.—(1) distress after 21 days' arrear, for arrears ; (2) entry and possession until payment, after 40 days' arrear, for arrears then due or becoming due during his possession ; and (3) also after 40 days' arrear, whether taking possession or not, by deed to demise the land charged to a trustee for a term by mortgage, sale or demise or by any other reasonable means, to raise and pay the annual sum and all arrears due or to become due. By the next section (45) of the same Act, any " quit-rent, chief-rent, " rent-charge or other annual sum issuing out of land," may be redeemed by the owner of the land or other person interested therein. *Vide* pp. 37, 38 *ante.*

14.—Where any right of grazing, sheepwalk, or other similar right is attached to land acquired by a County Council for the purposes of small holdings, the Council may attach any share of the right to any small holding in such manner and subject to such regulations as they think expedient (*a*).

(*a*) *See* sec. 4 and notes thereto. In Yorkshire, Cumberland, Wales, and Scotland this section is likely to have an important operation, but there are many parts of England where there will be little or no occasion for the exercise of the powers given by this section.

Letting of
land unsold,
and sale of
superfluous
or unsuit-
able land.

15.—(1) A County Council shall, if practicable, sell or let as small holdings, and in accordance with this Act, any land acquired under this Act, but if the Council are of opinion that any such land is not needed for, or is unsuitable for, small holdings, or cannot be sold or let under the foregoing provisions of this Act, or that some more suitable land is available, they may sell or let the land otherwise than under the said provisions, or exchange the land for other land more suitable for small holdings, and may pay or receive money for equality of exchange, and may erect such buildings or execute such other works as will in the opinion of the Council enable the land to be sold or let without loss.

(2) The Council may also, while any sale of a holding is pending in pursuance of this Act, temporarily let or manage the holding for such time and in such manner as they think expedient (*a*).

(3) Sections one hundred and twenty-eight to one hundred and thirty-two of the Lands Clauses Con-

8 & 9 Vict.
c. 18.

solidation Act, 1845 (relating to the right of pre-emption of superfluous lands) shall apply upon any sale in pursuance of this section before any such buildings or works as aforesaid are erected or executed on the land proposed to be sold, but save as aforesaid the provisions of the Lands Clauses Consolidation Act, 1845, with respect to the sale of superfluous lands shall not apply (*b*).

(*a*) The powers conferred by these two subsections are ancillary to the general power of acquisition of land for the purposes of the Small Holdings Act which the County Council possesses by virtue of sec. 1. These subsidiary powers enable the Council to carry out their dealings with land in the most effective and economical manner.

Sec. 16.

Letting of land unsold, and sale of superfluous or unsuitable land.

(*b*) For the text and a full explanation of secs. 128, 129 and 130 of 8 & 9 Vict. c. 18, *see* WOOLF and MIDDLETON on *Compensation;* CRIPPS on *Compensation*, chap. xix.

16.—(1) Where a County Council provide small holdings, they may delegate, with or without restrictions, the powers of the County Council under this Act with respect to the adaption of land for any holdings, and the sale, letting, and management of any holdings, to a committee (*a*) consisting of—

Provisions as to management of holdings.

> The county councillor representing the electoral division in which the holdings are situate ; and
>
> Two other members of the County Council ; and
>
> Two of the allotment managers (if any) under the Allotments Act, 1887, for the parish or area in which the holdings are situate selected by those managers, or if there are no allotment managers, two persons appointed in manner provided by that Act for the appointment of allotment managers (*b*) ; or

50 & 51 Vict. c. 48.

> If the holdings are situate within the limits of a municipal borough, then, instead of the persons selected or appointed as aforesaid, two members of the borough council ;

and in the construction of this Act references to the County Council shall, in their application to the powers so delegated, include any such committee. Provided that a County Council shall not under this section delegate any powers of making or levying a rate or of borrowing money (*c*).

Sec. 16.

Provisions
as to man-
agement of
holdings.
51 & 52 Vict.
c. 41.

(2) The Local Government Act, 1888, shall apply to any committee appointed under this section as if it were appointed under that Act (*d*).

(*a*) There are, therefore, two kinds of committee appointable for the purposes of the Small Holdings Act, viz.: (1) the committee which, by sec. 5, all County Councils, except the Councils of county-boroughs, are bound to nominate for the purpose of considering whether the Act ought to be put into working ; and (2) the committee which *may* (not *shall*) be appointed under sec. 16 (1). In other words, all the practical business under the Act, save the powers of making or levying a rate, or of borrowing money, may be delegated to a committee. This will be found a great convenience in actual practice.

(*b*) *See* 50 & 51 Vict. c. 48, sec. 6 (3), and sec. 9. The sanitary authority appoints and removes allotment managers of land acquired under this Act of 1887. Such managers may consist either partly of members of the sanitary authority, and partly of other persons, or wholly of other persons, provided that such other persons are contributors to the rate out of which the expenses under the Act are paid. By sec. 9, however, when allotments have been provided for a parish in any *rural* district, a petition to the sanitary authority may be presented by not less than one-sixth of the electors of allotment managers in the parish, asking for the election of allotment managers, and thereupon the sanitary authority must order an election. The managers so elected supersede those nominated by the sanitary authority.

(*c*) *See* 51 & 52 Vict. c. 41, secs. 28 and 81 (3). *Vide* STEPHEN and MILLER's *County Council Compendium*, p. 80.

(*d*) *Ibid.*, secs. 81 & 82. *See* also 45 & 46 Vict. c. 50, sec. 22. 51 & 52 Vict. c. 41, sec. 82 (2) provides that " every committee " shall report its proceedings to the Council by whom it was " appointed, *but to the extent to which the Council so direct*, the " acts and proceedings of the committee shall not be required by " the provisions of the Municipal Corporations Act, 1882, to be " submitted to the Council for their approval."

/ DEC 1920

PART II.

LOANS BY COUNTY COUNCILS TO TENANTS PURCHASING SMALL HOLDINGS.

17.—(1) Where the tenant of a small holding has agreed with his landlord for the purchase of the holding, the County Council of the county in which the holding or any part of it is situate may, if they think fit, advance to the tenant on the security of the holding an amount not exceeding four-fifths of the purchase-money thereof (*a*).

(2) The provisions of this Act with respect to the purchase money secured by a charge on a small holding sold by a County Council, and with respect to any small holding so sold, shall apply to an advance made and a holding purchased under this section, as if the advance was the purchase-money (*b*), save that the County Council shall not guarantee the title of the purchaser of the holding (*c*).

(3) No advance shall be made by a County Council under this section, unless they are satisfied that the title to the holding is good, that the sale is made in good faith, and that the price is reasonable (*d*).

Power of County Council to advance money for purchase of small holding.

(*a*) This restriction as to four-fifths of the amount agreed to be paid by the tenant to the selling landlord is analogous to the rule observed by persons advancing trust-moneys upon mortgage. It answers the same purpose, viz., to provide against any diminution in the value of the security in time to come ; and, in the case of the County Council, it is also a safeguard against imposition.

(*b*) *Vide* sec. 6, *ante.*

(*c*) There seems to be a curious mistake here. In the original draft of the bill there was a clause (sub-clause 7 of clause 6) providing that "the Council shall guarantee the title of the purchaser, and the remedy of any person claiming by a title paramount to the title of the Council shall be in damages only." This sub-clause was, however, afterwards struck out, and the words "save that the County Council shall not guarantee the title of the purchaser of the holding" ought, therefore, to have been struck out also.

(*d*) The conditions to be satisfied are, therefore, three in number, viz. : the title must be found to be a good one ; the application of the purchasing tenant must be made in good faith ; and the price must be reasonable. The above section does not direct the Council to register under the Land Transfer Act (*see* sec. 10, *ante*) ; but there seems to be nothing against this being done, especially as the Council are, under sec. 17 (3), to investigate the title before advancing the money.

The whole of the above section constitutes one of the most important and valuable provisions in the Act. By enabling what are called *sitting tenants* to become purchasers under this Act, the Legislature has carried the principle of the measure to its widest limit in this direction ; and it is hoped that many tenants will avail themselves of the provisions of this section and thus become cultivating owners.

PART III.

SUPPLEMENTAL.

18.—(1) A County Council shall not acquire land under this Act save at such price that, in the opinion of the Council, all expenses incurred by the Council in relation to the land will be recouped out of the purchase-money for the land sold by the Council, or in the case of land let, out of the rent, and shall fix the purchase-money or rent at such reasonable amount as will, in their opinion, guard them against loss (*a*).

(2) A County Council shall not take any proceedings under this Act whereby the charge for the time being on the county rate, for the purposes of this Act, including the annual payments in respect of the loans raised for those purposes, is, in the opinion of the Council, likely to exceed in any one year the amount produced by a rate of a penny in the pound, and, where the said charge at any time is equal or nearly equal to that amount, no further land shall be purchased in pursuance of this Act until the charge has been decreased so as to admit of the further purchase without the charge exceeding the said amount (*b*).

(*a*) *See* next sec. as to borrowing powers of Council.

(*b*) This is a valuable provision, and prevents any unfair or capricious exercise of the powers conferred by the Act. It is not the intention of the framers of the new legislation to provide

5

land for a section of the community at the expense of the whole body public.

Borrowing powers and expenses.

19.—(1) A County Council may borrow money for the purposes of this Act in accordance with the Local Government Act, 1888 (*a*), or, if the Council of a county-borough, with the Public Health Act, 1875 (*b*), except that any money so borrowed shall, notwithstanding anything in either of those Acts, be repaid within such period not exceeding fifty years as the Council, with the consent of the Local Government Board, determine in each case. Provided that money borrowed under this Act shall not be reckoned as part of the total debt of a county for the purpose of section sixty-nine, subsection two, of the Local Government Act, 1888 (*c*).

51 & 52 Vict. c. 41.

38 & 39 Vict. c. 55.

38 & 39 Vict. c. 69.

(2) The Public Works Loan Commissioners (*d*) may, in manner provided by the Public Works Loans Act, 1875, lend any money which may be borrowed by a County Council for the purposes of this Act.

(3) Every loan by the Public Works Loan Commissioners in pursuance of this Act shall bear such rate of interest, not less than three pounds two shillings and sixpence per cent. per annum, as the Treasury may authorise as being in their opinion sufficient to enable such loans to be made without loss to the Exchequer (*e*).

(4) Any capital money received by a County Council in payment or discharge of purchase-money for land sold by them, or in repayment of an advance made by them, shall be applied, with the sanction of the Local Government Board, either in repayment of

debt or for any other purpose for which capital money
may be applied (*f*).

(5) The expenses incurred by the Council of a
county-borough under this Act shall be defrayed out
of the borough fund or borough rate, and any money
borrowed by such a Council shall be borrowed on the
security of the borough fund or borough rate (*g*).

(*a*) A County Council borrows money by virtue of sec. 79 of
the Local Government Act, 1888. *See* hereon STEPHEN and
MILLER'S *County Council Compendium*, pp. 94–97 ; GLEN'S
County Government, p. 243 *et seq.*

(*b*) The following are the provisions of the Public Health
Act, 1875, with respect to borrowing, viz.—Sections 233, 234,
236, 237, 238, 239, 242, 243, 296, 297, and 298 ; Schedule IV.,
Forms H. and I. The Local Authorities Loans Acts are—38 &
39 Vict. c. 89 ; 39 & 40 Vict. c. 31 ; 41 Vict. c. 18 ; 42 & 43
Vict. c. 77 ; 44 & 45 Vict. c. 38 ; 45 & 46 Vict. c. 62 ; 46 &
47 Vict. c. 42.

(*c*) This subsection is as follows : " (2) Provided that where
" the total debt of the County Council, after deducting the amount
" of any sinking-fund, exceeds, or if [after] the proposed loan is
" borrowed will exceed, the amount of one-tenth of the annual
" rateable value of the rateable property in the county, ascertained
" according to the standard or basis for the county rate, the
" amount shall not be borrowed except in pursuance of a pro-
" visional order made by the Local Government Board and
" sanctioned by Parliament." With regard to provisional orders,
see 51 & 52 Vict. c. 41, sec. 87.

(*d*) These Commissioners are regulated by the following Acts :
38 & 39 Vict. c. 89 ; 41 & 42 Vict. c. 18 ; 42 & 43 Vict. c. 77 ;
44 & 45 Vict. c. 38 ; 45 & 46 Vict. c. 62 ; 46 & 47 Vict. c. 42 ;
48 & 49 Vict. c. 65.

(*e*) It should be noted that there is nothing in this section
which prevents a Council from getting the money required

Sec. 19.

Borrowing powers and expenses.

from any other source than the Public Works Loans Commissioners, if the Council find that it may be borrowed elsewhere with advantage.

    (*f*) *Cf.* 51 & 52 Vict. c. 41, sec. 69.

    (*g*) *Vide* LUMLEY's *Public Health*, 3rd ed., p. 307.

Definitions.

20.—For the purposes of this Act—

The expressions "agriculture" and "cultivation" shall include horticulture and the use of land for any purpose of husbandry, inclusive of the keeping or breeding of live stock, poultry or bees, and the growth of fruit, vegetables, and the like :

The expression "county" shall mean the area under the authority of a County Council :

The expression "County Council" shall include the Council of a county borough, and the expression "electoral division" in its application to a county borough divided into wards shall mean ward, and in its application to a county borough the expression "county rate" shall mean the borough rate or borough fund :

The expression "county elector" shall include "burgess."

In this Act, and in the enactments incorporated with this Act, the expression "land" shall include any right or easement in or over land.

Modifications of Act and application to Scotland.

8 & 9 Vict. c. 19.

21.—In the application of this Act to Scotland—

(1) A reference to any sections of the Lands Clauses Consolidation Act, 1845, shall be construed as a reference to the corresponding sections of the Lands Clauses Consolidation (Scotland) Act, 1845 :

(2) A reference to the Local Government Act, 1888, shall be construed as a reference to the Local Government (Scotland) Act, 1889 :

(3) The Secretary for Scotland shall be substituted for the Local Government Board :

(4) The expression "county rate" shall mean the general purposes rate leviable by a County Council :

(5) The expression "devise" shall mean *mortis causa* disposition :

(6) The expression "easement" shall mean servitude :

(7) The references to county boroughs shall not apply :

(8) The expression "county elector" shall have the same meaning as in the Local Government (Scotland) Act, 1889.

Sec. 21.
Modifica-tions of Act and appli-cation to Scotland. 52 & 53 Vict. c. 50.

22.—With respect to the unpaid purchase-money for a small holding under this Act, the following provisions shall have effect in Scotland in lieu of sub-sections four and five of section six of this Act :—

Modifica-tions with respect to regulations as to purchase-money in Scotland.

(1) A portion, representing not more than one-fourth of the purchase-money, may, if the County Council think fit, be converted into a perpetual rent-charge which shall be a real burden affecting the holding, redeemable at any time at the option of the purchaser in accordance with tables fixed by the County Council, and the certificate of the county clerk that the redemption-money has been paid shall, without any other instrument, operate

Sec. 22.

Modifications with respect to regulations as to purchase-money in Scotland.

as an extinction of the rent-charge, and the registration of such certificate in the register of sasines shall be equivalent to the registration of a discharge of the said rent-charge:

(2) The residue (if any) of the purchase-money shall be secured by a bond which shall be a charge on the holding in favour of the County Council, and shall either be repaid by half-yearly instalments of principal with such interest and within such term not exceeding fifty years from the date of the sale as may be agreed on with the Council, or shall, if the purchaser so requires, be repaid with such interest and within such term by a terminable annuity payable by half-yearly instalments. The amount for the time being unpaid may at any time be discharged, and any such terminable annuity may at any time be redeemed in accordance with tables fixed by the County Council. A certificate by the county clerk that the whole of the said residue has been paid, or that such terminable annuity has been redeemed, shall, without any other instrument, operate as a discharge of the said residue and extinction of the said terminable annuity, as the case may be, and the registration of such certificate in the register of sasines shall be equivalent to the registration of a discharge of the said bond.

23.—In Scotland the County Council shall cause to be prepared and duly registered all deeds, writs, and instruments necessary for completing the titles of the

purchaser of a small holding, and for securing the with small holdings in Scotland.
payment of any unpaid purchase-money, and shall
include in the purchase-money the cost so incurred, or
to be incurred, according to scales set forth in tables
fixed by the County Council.

Provided that—

(1) the County Council, if they think fit, may appoint
a person duly qualified (in the opinion of the
sheriff) to carry out the provisions of this section,
and shall assign to him such salary or other
remuneration as they may determine ; and

(2) the County Council shall not be liable for any
expenses incurred by the purchaser of a small
holding for legal or other advice or assistance
rendered to him on his own employment.

Sections ten, twelve, and thirteen of this Act shall
not apply to Scotland.

24.—A committee of a County Council appointed Modifications as regards management of holdings in Scotland.
under this Act with respect to the adaptation of land
for small holdings, and the sale, letting, and management of the holdings, shall, in Scotland, consist of—

The county councillor representing the electoral
division in which the holding are situate ; and

Two other members of the County Council ; and

Two persons elected triennially by the county
electors in the electoral division aforesaid, in
accordance with such regulations as the Secretary
for Scotland may from time to time prescribe,
whether preliminary or incidental to such election,
and for applying to such election any enactments

Sec. 24.

Modifications as regards management of holdings in Scotland.

as to offences at the election of county councillors and for supplying casual vacancies on the committee ; or

If the holdings are situate within the limits of any burgh, then, instead of the persons elected as aforesaid, two town councillors or commissioners, as the case may be, to be appointed for that purpose by the Town Council or Commissioners of such burgh.

Extent of Act.

25.—This Act shall not apply to Ireland.

Commencement of Act.

26.—This Act shall come into operation on the first day of October, one thousand eight hundred and ninety-two.

Short title.

27.—This Act may be cited as the Small Holdings Act, 1892.

APPENDIX A.

THE SELECT COMMITTEE ON SMALL HOLDINGS.

THIS Committee was re-appointed, by an order of the House of Commons made on the 27th day of March, 1890, " to inquire into the facilities which exist for the creation of small holdings in land in Great Britain ; whether, either in connection with an improved system of local government or otherwise, those facilities may be extended ; whether in recent years there has been any diminution in the number of small owners and culti-vators of land, and whether there is any evidence to show that such diminution is due to legislation."

SUMMARY OF CONCLUSIONS OF THE COMMITTEE.

1. That the extension of a system of small holdings is a matter of national importance, both in the interests of the rural popula-tion and also as adding to the security of property generally.

2. That the intervention of the Legislature is called for by the special circumstances of the case, and is justified by considera-tions affecting the well-being of the whole community.

3. That there has been until quite recently a considerable diminution both in small agricultural ownerships and tenancies.

4. That this diminution has been due—

(a) In the case of small tenancies, chiefly to economic

causes, and especially to the policy of consolidating farms, which prevailed largely till within the last few years, but has now practically ceased.

(b) In the case of small ownerships, partly to economic causes, and especially to the low return for capital afforded by investment in land, and partly to the indirect effects of legislation, more especially of the laws of settlement and entail, and the law and practice with regard to enclosures.

5. That no special facilities are afforded by existing legislation for the creation of small holdings.

6. That it is desirable that any system of small holdings should be graduated upwards from simple allotments or cottage-gardens to farms of 50 acres or £50 in annual value.

7. That in order to meet the case of ordinary labourers, and to provide a ladder by which they may gradually raise themselves to the position of small owners, they recommend that in conjunction with facilities for purchase the local authorities should have power to let land in small holdings not exceeding 10 acres.

8. That a system of ownership, however qualified, in the case of small holdings is preferable to any system of tenancy, except in the case of very small holdings.

9. That it is desirable to confer upon local authorities power to purchase land for the purpose of creating small cultivating ownerships, and to borrow the money from the Public Works Loan Commission.

10. That land in sufficient quantities for the purpose can be obtained by voluntary agreement, and that it is not necessary at present to resort to compulsory powers.

11. That it is essential that the purchasers of small holdings should provide in cash a proportion of the purchase-money not less than one-fifth or one-fourth of the whole.

12. That the balance of the purchase-money, after payment of

the proportion required in cash, should be lent by the local authority, at a rate of interest so arranged as to allow of its periodic reduction until it is reduced to a small proportion of the original charge, when it would remain as a perpetual feu or quit-rent of small amount.

13. That where small holdings are created by the local authority, subletting and subdivision of the holding should be prohibited.

14. That the local authority should have power at any time to resume possession of the land for public purposes or for building land, on payment of full compensation, based on its value as an agricultural occupation.

15. That any legislation on the subject should apply to the whole of Great Britain.

16. That in the first instance the advance of public money to local authorities for the purpose of creating small holdings should not exceed a total sum of £5,000,000, and that no local authority should be authorised to pledge the local rates for any sum which should involve an annual charge in the shape of interest and sinking fund exceeding 1d. in the £ on the rateable value of the district of such local authority.

APPENDIX B.

PETITIONS TO COUNTY COUNCIL UNDER SEC. 5 (2) OF THE ACT.

THE reader will observe, upon referring to sec. 5 (2) of the Small Holdings Act, that any county elector or electors (and in a county-borough, any burgess or burgesses) *may present a petition* to the County Council (including the Council of a county-borough) "alleging that there is a demand for small holdings in " the county, and praying that [Part I.] of the Act may be put " into operation." This petition, which need not be in any particular form, will be referred to the committee, appointed under sec. 5, " who, on being satisfied that the petition is pre-" sented in good faith and on reasonable grounds, shall forthwith " cause an inquiry into the circumstances to be made, and shall " report the result to the Council." The Council, it may be added, will not be bound by this report ; but it is believed that County Councils will seldom refuse to ratify the conclusions at which the committee may have arrived.

Persons making a petition will do well to place before the County Council all facts within their knowledge which go to prove the existence of a demand for small holdings. Petitioners should likewise state, as nearly as possible, the size or sizes of the suggested small holdings ; and it will be expedient to make specific offers to the Council to purchase or hire such or such a quantity of land, and to say how much would be given for pur-chase or hire thereof. If it be known that any particular land-owner has land suitable for small holdings, which he is willing to sell, a letter should, if possible, be obtained from him stating the area, situation, and price of the said land. Purchasers and hirers of land must undertake to cultivate the land themselves.

The Council are required by the Act to " fix the purchase-money " or rent at such reasonable amount as will, in their opinion, " guard them against loss." Hence persons seeking to buy or hire land must be prepared to give a price or pay a rent which will enable the Council to recoup themselves. It would be desirable, furthermore, to obtain the support of leading people in the neighbourhood to the petition, as is done in the case of allotments. It will be allowable, also, for public associations and public meetings to support petitions to the Council.

The following are suggested as being proper forms of petition :—

FORM OF PETITION No. I.

To the County Council of the Administrative County of East Suffolk.

We, the persons whose signatures are appended hereto, being county electors of the county of East Suffolk, hereby beg to represent to the East Suffolk County Council that there is a demand for small holdings [in the parish of Wrentham, which is situate in the Kessingland electoral division of North Suffolk], or, [in the Kessingland electoral division of North Suffolk] in the said county of East Suffolk, and we respectfully request that Part I. of the Small Holdings Act, 1892, may be put into force.

(Here follow the names, occupations, and abodes of the petitioners.)

FORM OF PETITION No. II.

To the County Council of the County Borough of Kingston-upon-Hull.

We, the persons whose signatures are appended hereto, being burgesses of the county-borough of Kingston-upon-Hull, hereby beg to represent to the Council of the said county-borough that there is a demand for small holdings in the X. ward of the said county-borough, and we respectfully request that Part I. of the Small Holdings Act, 1892, may be put into force.

(Here follow the names, occupations, and abodes of the petitioners.)

APPENDIX C.

LAND REGISTRY.

LAND TRANSFER ACT 1875, AND SMALL HOLDINGS ACT, 1892.

RULES.

I, the Right Honourable Hardinge Stanley, Baron Halsbury, Lord High Chancellor of Great Britain, with the advice and assistance of Robert Hallett Holt, Barrister-at-Law, Registrar of the Land Registry, by virtue and in pursuance of the Land Transfer Act, 1875, and the Small Holdings Act, 1892, and of all other powers and authorities enabling in that behalf, do make the following Rules for the purpose of carrying the said Acts into execution.

Dated this 9th day of August, 1892.

HALSBURY, C.

ROBERT HALLETT HOLT.

LAND REGISTRY.

RULES UNDER SECTION 10 OF THE SMALL HOLDINGS ACT, 1892.

PRELIMINARY.

1. In these Rules the Small Holdings Act, 1892, is referred to as the Act.

PART I.

REGISTRATION OF LAND ON ACQUISITION BY A COUNTY COUNCIL.

I.—*Generally.*

2. Application by a County Council for registration as proprietor, with absolute title, of land acquired in pursuance of the Act, shall be made in Form 1, or to the like effect, and shall be signed by the clerk or the solicitor to, or some other responsible officer of, the Council, and shall be accompanied by a map of the land (prepared according to Rule 6 of the Land Registry Rules, 1889), the conveyance to the Council, and a statutory declaration by the solicitor of the Council, or such other solicitor as may have been employed by them in the purchase, in Form 2, or to the like effect.

3. If the Council have purchased in consideration of a fee-farm or other rent secured by a condition of re-entry or otherwise, whether under section 13 of the Act or under section 10 of the

Lands Clauses Consolidation Act, 1845, or if the land is subject to any incumbrance, or if it be known that the mines and minerals are excepted, the fact shall be stated and short particulars given in the statutory declaration aforesaid.

4. On receipt of the application, the aforesaid statutory declaration shall be filed and referred to on the register, and the registrar shall register the County Council as proprietors of the land for the purposes of the Act, with an absolute title, if satisfied that they have a good holding title, or, if not so satisfied, he shall register the County Council provisionally, pending further investigation, with such other title as is authorised by the Land Transfer Act, 1875 ; and in the latter case the purchasers from the County Council shall, pending the completion of the absolute registration, have the benefit of the title possessed by the County Council at the time of their provisional registration, and on the registration of such purchasers a note shall be made on the register accordingly.

5. The completion of the registration with absolute title shall be proceeded with, or may be allowed to stand over for such period and subject to such conditions as the registrar shall direct.

6. At any time before the actual registration of the title as absolute, any person may lodge a caution against such absolute registration being made, similar to and with the like effect as a caution against entry of land on the register.

7. The title of the County Council may be registered as absolute at such time after the appearance of the advertisement of the application as the registrar shall think fit.

8. In the event of any sale of a small holding by the County Council, being either a part or the whole of the land comprised in a title, during the period between the provisional registration and the completion of registration with an absolute title, the County Council shall, nevertheless, proceed to complete the registration with absolute title of the whole of the land comprised in the provisional registration, and upon such completion the purchaser of the small holding shall be registered as proprietor with an absolute title of the purchased land.

II.—*Investigation of Title under Conveyancing Counsel outside the Office.*

9. If at any time, either before or after the purchase of land, and either before or after the leaving of a formal application for registration, the County Council desire to have the title investigated through the registry with a view to registration with absolute title, they may apply to the registrar for a reference of the title to any land they have purchased, or are about to purchase, to a conveyancing counsel, and the registrar shall, if he think proper, refer them to such conveyancing counsel (of not less than 10 years' standing) as he shall think fit.

10. The title shall be investigated by such counsel, and the conveyance (if not already settled) shall be settled by him under the instructions of the County Council, and shall describe the property by reference to the ordnance map.

11. If the application for registration by the County Council is made after the execution of the conveyance, they shall leave with the application a report on their title signed by the conveyancing counsel by whom the investigation was made.

12. Such report shall state whether or not the title of the County Council appears to be a good holding title, and whether or not there are any qualifications, incumbrances, conditions, exceptions, or other matters affecting it which ought to be entered on the register, and, if any, the details thereof.

13. The registrar may act on such report, and may register the title as absolute or qualified accordingly, but if it appear to the registrar that the title, though open to objection, is one the holding under which will not be disturbed, he may register the same as absolute, or otherwise proceed under the 17th section of the Land Transfer Act, 1875.

14. Where the title has already been investigated by any such conveyancing counsel as aforesaid, the County Council may request that the reference be made to such counsel if the registrar so think fit.

6

15. Where the sale has been completed without the opinion of such conveyancing counsel as aforesaid being taken, the title may be referred and proceeded with in the same manner as above prescribed as soon as the application for registration is left in the office.

PART II.

REGISTRATION OF SALES BY COUNTY COUNCIL FOR SMALL HOLDINGS.

16. On a sale of a small holding by the County Council, the instrument of transfer shall be in Form 3.

17. Where the whole of the purchase-money is not paid on completion, the purchaser shall execute a charge in Form 4, 5, or 6, with such additions and modification as the circumstances may require.

18. Such charge, so executed, shall be entered on the register, and shall (subject to the provisions of the Act) operate in all respects as a charge made by a registered proprietor of the land, and may be dealt with on the register accordingly.

19. An entry shall be made on the register to the effect that the land was originally acquired under the Act, giving also the date of the sale by the County Council, and showing that the land is subject generally to such of the restrictions and conditions imposed by the Act as may for the time being be subsisting.

20. Such entry may be modified or removed with the consent of the County Council, and on production of a certificate signed by the clerk or solicitor, or other responsible officer of the said Council, to the effect that the land is no longer subject to the conditions contained in section 9 of the Act, or that the requirements of section 11 of the Act have been complied with respectively.

21. The cost of the land certificate to be issued to the purchaser from the County Council shall, for the purpose of section 6, subsection (1) of the Act, be included in the costs of registration of title.

PART III.

22. On any sale made by the County Council under section 9 of the Act, the County Council shall have power to transfer the land, and the instrument of transfer shall be in Form 7 or to the like effect.

23. The provisions hereinbefore contained as to the creation of incumbrances by the first purchaser of a small holding shall apply to any such sale.

24. The transferee shall be registered as proprietor, and suitable entries and cancellations shall be made on the register according to the terms of the transfer, and no evidence shall be required by the registrar as to the happening of any of the events mentioned in the said section 9 as giving rise to the powers of the County Council, or the fulfilment of any of the provisions in that section contained.

PART IV.

25. On the death of the sole proprietor, or of the survivor of several joint registered proprietors of a small holding, the registrar may enter the executor or administrator (if any) as proprietor in the place of the deceased proprietor without regard to the beneficial title.

26. The application for such registration shall be in Form 8.

27. In the exercise of his power as registered proprietor of the land, such executor or administrator shall be a trustee for all persons beneficially interested, and (except for purposes of registered dealings for value with the land) the registration of the executor or administrator shall not affect the beneficial ownership of the land.

28. Production of the probate or letters of administration shall be sufficient proof of the death of the proprietor, and of the execution and validity of the will, or the fact of the intestacy.

29. A statutory declaration of identity in Form 9 or to the like effect shall be the only additional evidence required.

30. Where the will is not proved, or no administration is taken out, the registrar shall proceed as prescribed by section 41 of the Land Transfer Act, 1875.

PART V.

LOCAL OFFICERS.

31. The registrar may, on the application of the County Council, appoint suitable persons as local registrars for the purposes of section 10 of the Act.

32. Every person so appointed shall be either a barrister or a solicitor, or an officer of the County Council, or a district registrar of the High Court, or a registrar of the County Court, or a registrar of an existing local deed registry.

33. The local registrar shall supply information to the owners of small holdings and other persons in regard to all matters connected with registration and transfer of land under the Act, and shall give all necessary assistance in the preparation of instruments for registration and transfer under the Act.

34. The remuneration of the local registrar shall be provided by the County Council, and shall be regulated in such manner as they shall determine.

35. A reasonable contribution to the remuneration of the local registrar may, for the purposes of section 6, subsection (1) of the Act, be included in the cost of registration of title.

36. The persons appointed as hereinbefore mentioned may be removed by the registrar at any time for incompetence or failure to perform their duties in a satisfactory manner, or (on the application of the County Council) on the ground that the amount of business is insufficient to require such local assistance.

PART VI.

MISCELLANEOUS.

37. Where the land purchased by the County Council is already registered with an indefeasible title under the Land Registry Act, 1862, or with an absolute title under the Land Transfer Act, 1875, the proceedings under these Rules shall be modified in such manner as the registrar may deem convenient.

38. Every instrument of transfer or charge duly executed relating to a small holding shall (so far as consistent with the Act) take effect as a conveyance or mortgage by deed, and the provisions of the Conveyancing Act, 1881, shall take effect accordingly, except as varied or negatived in the instrument or by these Rules.

39. So long as land is registered as subject to the Act, no transfer (including a transfer by the registered proprietor of a charge) or charge shall be registered without the consent of the County Council, testified by their concurring in the execution thereof.

40. On any sale by the registered proprietor of a charge, the instrument of transfer shall be deemed to have been made in professed exercise of the power of sale (if any) implied in the charge.

41. On any transfer for value of land, made by the registered proprietor of a registered charge or incumbrance conferring a

power of sale, it shall be assumed that the transfer is made in exercise of the power, and that the land transferred is sold free from the charge, and from all charges registered subsequently thereto.

42. No purchaser of land, provisionally registered under these Rules, or registered with an absolute title, shall (in the absence of express stipulation to the contrary) require any further title beyond that to be obtained by an inspection of the register, or a certified extract from, or copy of the register (to be furnished at his expense), and a statutory declaration (at the like expense) as to the existence or otherwise of matters which are declared by section 18 of the Land Transfer Act, 1875, not to be incumbrances within the meaning of that Act.

43. In applying the 3rd and 6th subsections of section 83 of the Land Transfer Act of 1875 to small holdings, the word "registrar" shall be substituted for the word "court."

44. Any land on which a County Council has advanced money under section 19 of the Act may, with the consent of the County Council, be registered, provisionally or otherwise, in like manner and with the like effect as hereinbefore provided with respect to land originally acquired by the County Council for the purposes of the Act.

45. Where land is sold or exchanged by the County Council under section 15 of the Act, the instrument of transfer shall contain additions in Form 10 or to the like effect.

46. On receipt of such transfer, the registrar shall register the transferee without further inquiry as to the fulfilment of the provisions of the said section, and shall cancel all references to the Act that may have been entered on the register and that no longer affect the land.

47. Except as varied by these Rules, the existing Rules made under the Land Transfer Act, 1875, shall apply to small holdings.

48. These Rules may be cited as The Land Registry (Small Holdings) Rules, 1892, and shall commence on the 1st of October, 1892.

SCHEDULE OF FORMS.

***

FORM 1.

APPLICATION BY A COUNTY COUNCIL FOR FIRST REGISTRATION AS PROPRIETORS OF LAND.

LAND REGISTRY.

LAND TRANSFER ACT, 1875, AND SMALL HOLDINGS ACT, 1892.

No. of title.

The County Council of
apply to be registered as proprietors with absolute title of the land
shown and edged with red on the accompanying map marked
, which land is also comprised in the
accompanying conveyance marked ,
and is also referred to in the accompanying statutory declaration
marked .

Dated the of 189 .

(Signature of the clerk, solicitor, &c., to
the Council.)

The address for service of the said Council is at

FORM 2.

STATUTORY DECLARATION TO ACCOMPANY APPLICATION IN FORM 1.

LAND REGISTRY.

LAND TRANSFER ACT, 1875, AND SMALL HOLDINGS ACT, 1892.

No. of title

In the matter of the application of the County Council of

I,

of

solicitor, do solemnly and sincerely declare as follows :—

I acted for the above-named Council in the purchase of the land shown and edged with red on the map marked   now produced and shown to me. As such solicitor I examined the vendor's title in manner following [here state particulars of examination, length of title shown, name of counsel (if any) employed, special conditions (if any), comparison of abstract, name and address of vendor and vendor's solicitor, &c., &c.]

The investigation so made was, in my opinion, as full an investigation of the vendor's title as was reasonably possible and suitable under the circumstances of the case.

I (or the said counsel where employed) advised that the title was a good holder's title, and I know of nothing which would lead me to suppose that there is any adverse claim in existence against it.

The said land has been duly conveyed to the said Council (subject to the incumbrances, leases, conditions, the farm rent, &c., &c., set forth in the Schedule hereto).

From the above consideration I am able to state that the said Council have a good holding title to the said land (subject as aforesaid).

THE SCHEDULE.

And I make, &c.

FORM 3.

INSTRUMENT OF TRANSFER ON A SALE OF A SMALL HOLDING BY THE COUNTY COUNCIL.

LAND REGISTRY.

LAND TRANSFER ACT, 1875, AND SMALL HOLDINGS ACT, 1892.

No. of title

of   189 . In consideration of £   [and *if so* of
the perpetual rent-charge of £   secured by instrument of
even date herewith *or otherwise as provided by section* 6 *of the Act*].
The County Council of   hereby transfer
to
of
all the land [shown and edged with red on the map marked
                sealed by the said Council, and also signed by or
on behalf of the said transferee, being part of the land] comprised
in the title above referred to for the purposes of a small holding
under the Small Holdings Act, 1892.

The
Seal of the
County
Council.

FORM 4.

PERPETUAL RENT-CHARGE TO SECURE PART OF PURCHASE-MONEY FOR A SMALL HOLDING.

LAND REGISTRY.

LAND TRANSFER ACT, 1875, AND SMALL HOLDINGS ACT, 1892.

No. of title

              of   189   . To secure
£   , part of the purchase-money of the land [shown
and edged with red on the map marked   , signed by
me, being part of the land] comprised in the title above referred to
I,
of
hereby charge the said land with the payment to the County Council
of
of a perpetual yearly rent-charge of £
payable on the   of
the   of   in every year.

The charge will be printed on a double folio, similarly to charges made under the Land Registry Rules of 1889, to be obtained at the registry.

N.B.—Sec. 44 of Conveyancing Act, 1881, combined with Rule 38, gives necessary powers of distress and entry.

FORM 5.

Charge Repayable by Half-Yearly Instalments to Secure Part of Purchase-Money for a Small Holding.

LAND REGISTRY.

Land Transfer Act, 1875, and Small Holdings Act, 1892.

No. of title

of   189   .   To secure £   , part of the
purchase-money of the land [shown and edged with red on the
map marked   , signed by me, being part of the land]
comprised in the title above referred to, I
of
hereby charge the said land with the payment to the County Council
of   of the sum of £   payable
by the   half-yearly instalments of £
with interest at   per cent. per annum on the amount for the
time being remaining unpaid on the   of
and the   of   in every year.

The charge will be printed on a double folio, similarly to charges
under the Land Registry Rules of 1889, to be obtained at the
registry.

N.B. All further necessary powers are in secs. 22 to 28 of the Land Transfer
Act and Conveyancing Act, 1881, secs. 19 to 22, and Rules 38 and 40.

FORM 6.

TERMINABLE ANNUITY TO SECURE PART OF PURCHASE-MONEY FOR A SMALL HOLDING.

LAND REGISTRY.

LAND TRANSFER ACT, 1875, AND SMALL HOLDINGS ACT, 1892.

No. of title

of   189 . To secure £   , part of the
purchase-money of the land [shown and edged with red on the map
marked   signed by me, being part of the land] comprised
in the title above referred to, and interest thereon at   per cent.
per annum, I
                              of
hereby charge the said land with the payment to the County Council
of   of an annuity of £   for
years, payable half yearly on the   day of   and
the   of   in every year.

The charge will be printed on a double folio, similarly to charges
under the Land Registry Rules of 1889, to be obtained at the registry.

N.B.—Sec. 44 of Conveyancing Act, 1881, combined with Rule 38, gives
necessary powers of distress and entry.

FORM 7.

Instrument of Transfer on Sale by County Council under Section 9 of the Small Holdings Act, 1892.

LAND REGISTRY.

Land Transfer Act, 1875, and Small Holdings Act, 1892.

No. of title

of   189 . In consideration of £   and *if so* of the perpetual rent-charge of £   [secured by instrument of even date herewith, *or otherwise as provided by section 6 of the Act*], and by virtue and in pursuance of section 9 of the Small Holdings Act, 1892. The County Council of
                              hereby transfer to
                                    of
                                    the land comprised in the title above referred to [free from the charge (*s*) dated the   of
          18   , and the   of   18   ,
and the annuity dated the   of   18   ,
registered against the said title [as the case may be], and free from the conditions (*b*), (*c*), (*d*), &c., of subsection (1) of the said section 9 of the said Act.

Seal of the Council.

FORM 8.

APPLICATION FOR REGISTRATION OF THE EXECUTOR OR ADMINISTRATOR OF A DECEASED PROPRIETOR.

———————

LAND REGISTRY.

LAND TRANSFER ACT, 1875, AND SMALL HOLDINGS ACT, 1892.

No. of title

A. B., of
the executor [administrator] of C. D., of
deceased, the registered proprietor of the above title, hereby applies
for registration in his place.

Dated the   of   189 .

(Signature of executor [or administrator]
or his solicitor).

———————

FORM 9.

STATUTORY DECLARATION OF IDENTITY OF A TESTATOR OR INTESTATE.

LAND REGISTRY.

LAND TRANSFER ACT, 1875, AND SMALL HOLDINGS ACT, 1892.

No. of title

I   of
solemnly and sincerely
declare as follows —

I knew C. D.   of
the testator [intestate]
named in the probate [letters of administration] now produced
and shown to me marked   . The said C. D. was
to the best of my knowledge and belief the same person as the C. D.
of
[registered address]
named in the register under the title above referred to.

And I make, &c.

FORM 10.

ADDITIONS TO INSTRUMENT OF TRANSFER ON SALE UNDER SECTION 15 OF "THE SMALL HOLDINGS ACT."

(1.) After " In consideration of £   " add " and by " virtue and in pursuance of section 15 of the Small Holdings " Act, 1892."

(2.) At the end of the instrument add " to hold the same free " from all obligations and liabilities under or by reason of the " said Act."

LAND REGISTRY.

LAND TRANSFER ACT, 1875.

RULE.

I, the Right Honourable Hardinge Stanley, Baron Halsbury, Lord High Chancellor of Great Britain, with the concurrence of the Treasury, by virtue and in pursuance of the Land Transfer Act, 1875, and of all other powers and authorities enabling in that behalf, do determine that from the date of this Rule—

No *ad valorem* fee shall be chargeable on the registration of a caution or restriction containing a proviso that it shall cease to operate at the end of one year or less from the date of its registration ; but that this Rule shall not apply to a caution or restriction by way of renewal of any such caution or restriction as aforesaid, and that £1 shall be the minimum fee for registering any caution or restriction.

Dated this 8th day of August, 1892.

HALSBURY, *C.*

We certify that this Rule is made with the concurrence of the Treasury.

SIDNEY HERBERT.
W. H. WALROND.

7

LAND REGISTRY.

LAND REGISTRY ACT, 1862.

GENERAL ORDER.

With the sanction of the Right Honourable Hardinge Stanley, Baron Halsbury, Lord High Chancellor of Great Britain, I, Robert Hallett Holt, Barrister-at-Law, Registrar of the Land Registry, by virtue and in pursuance of the 25th and 26th Victoria. cap. 53, and all other powers and authorities enabling in that behalf, do determine that from the date of this Order—

No *ad valorem* fee shall be chargeable on the registration of a caveat or restriction containing a proviso that it shall cease to operate at the end of one year or less from the date of its registration ; but that this Rule shall not apply to a caution or restriction by way of renewal of any such caution or restriction as aforesaid, and that £1 shall be the minimum fee for registering any caution or restriction.

Dated this 8th day of August, 1892.

HALSBURY, *C.*
ROBERT HALLETT HOLT.

LAND REGISTRY.

LAND TRANSFER ACT, 1875, AND SMALL HOLDINGS ACT, 1892.

ORDER AS TO FEES.

RULE.

I, the Right Honourable Hardinge Stanley, Baron Halsbury, Lord High Chancellor of Great Britain, with the concurrence of the Treasury, by virtue and in pursuance of the Land Transfer Act, 1875, and the Small Holdings Act, 1892, and of all other powers and authorities enabling in that behalf, do determine that the fees to be paid in the Land Registry in respect of transactions under the last-mentioned Act shall be regulated as follows, namely :—

The fee for provisional registration (to be paid on leaving the application for registration) shall be the same as for an absolute title, but no fee shall be charged on the complete registration of the same as absolute.

The fee payable on the registration of a purchase of a small holding on first transfer from the County Council shall be ½d. in the £, and no registration fee shall be payable in respect of any charge made by such purchaser in favour of the County Council as part of the purchase arrangement if left for registration within three months of the registration of such purchaser.

The fee chargeable on the issue of a land certificate in respect of the first transfer of a small holding for a value exceeding £300* and not exceeding £1,000, if applied for within three months of the first registration of the purchaser, shall be 5s.

In all other respects the fee orders for the time being in force in the Land Registry shall apply.

Dated this 15th of August, 1892.

HALSBURY, C.

We certify that this Rule is made with the concurrence of the Treasury.

Signed $\begin{cases} \text{GEORGE J. GOSCHEN,} \\ \text{HERBERT EUSTACE MAXWELL.} \end{cases}$

---

* *No fee is payable for a land certificate by a transferee of land on a transfer not exceeding £300 in value.*

INDEX.

LIST

OF

LEGAL AND GENERAL BOOKS

PRINTED AND PUBLISHED

BY

WATERLOW & SONS LIMITED,

LAW, PARLIAMENTARY AND GENERAL
STATIONERS, PRINTERS, &c.,

85 & 86, LONDON WALL;

25, 26 & 27, GREAT WINCHESTER STREET;

FINSBURY STATIONERY WORKS, E.C.;

AND

49 & 50, PARLIAMENT STREET, S.W.,

ETC., ETC.,

LONDON.

LIST OF PUBLICATIONS.

THE AGRICULTURAL HOLDINGS (ENGLAND) ACT, 1883, with Notes and Forms, and a Summary of the Procedure. By J. W. JEUDWINE, of Lincoln's Inn, Barrister-at-Law. Second Edition, revised and enlarged. In cloth, 3s. 6d.

THE BANKERS', INSURANCE MANAGERS' AND AGENTS' MAGAZINE, —A first-class Monthly Financial Publication, and the recognised organ of communication for the Banking Interest. 1s. 6d. per number, or 21s. per annum, including two double numbers.

THE BANKING ALMANAC, DIRECTORY, AND DIARY.—A Year Book of Statistics and complete Banking Directory. The Edition for 1893 is the 49th year of publication of this invaluable book, which has long been patronized by the Bank of England and the Private and Joint Stock Banks throughout the Kingdom. Published annually in November. Cloth, lettered, 10s.

THE BANKRUPTCY ACT, 1883, with Introduction and Index. By His Honour Judge CHALMERS and E. HOUGH, of the Board of Trade. In boards, 2s. 6d.

THE BANKRUPTCY ACTS, 1883 TO 1890, with the General Rules, 1886 and 1890, Forms, Scales of Costs, Fees and Percentages, Board of Trade and Court Orders, Debtors' Act, 1869, Deeds of Arrangement Act, 1887, Rules as to Administration Orders, &c., and a Commentary thereon. By His Honour Judge CHALMERS, and E. HOUGH, Inspector in Bankruptcy, Board of Trade. Third Edition. In cloth, 21s.

THE BILLS OF EXCHANGE ACT, 1882.—An Act to Codify the Law relating to Bills of Exchange, Cheques, and Promissory Notes. With Comments and Explanatory Notes. By His Honour Judge CHALMERS. Seventh Edition. In cloth, 3s. 6d.

CHART OF THE BANKRUPTCY ACTS, 1883 and 1890 (Copyright), showing at a glance the Procedure from Act of Bankruptcy to Discharge. Revised in accordance with last Act and Rules. By R. T. HUNTER, Stockton-on-Tees. Price 1s. 6d. Mounted on Linen and Rollers, 3s.

A CODE OF CONTRACT LAW, relating to Sales of Goods of the value of £10 and upwards. A Handbook for the use of professional and business men. By HENRY J. PARRINGTON, of Middlesbrough, Solicitor. In cloth, 3s. 6d.

THE COMPUTATOR. A Treatise and Ready-Help for the young Banker's or Accountant's Clerk. With tables, &c. By A. WALKER. In cloth, 1s.

THE CRIMINAL LAW AMENDMENT ACT, 1885, with Preface and Commentary. By R. W. BURNIE, of the Middle Temple, Barrister-at-Law. In boards, 2s. 6d.

THE COUNTY COUNCIL COMPENDIUM ; or, DIGEST OF THE MUNICIPAL CORPORATIONS ACT, 1882; THE COUNTY ELECTORS AND LOCAL GOVERNMENT ACTS, 1888. Being a Treatise on the above Statutes and others re-enacted therein. With Copious Notes and Appendices, &c. Second Edition. By HENRY STEPHEN and HORACE E. MILLER, LL.B., Barristers-at-Law. In cloth, 21s.

THE COUNTY COUNCILLOR'S VADE-MECUM.—This book is intended for the use of persons desirous of becoming members of the County Councils who may be elected Councillors or Aldermen. It contains all details which it is necessary that a Candidate should know, and points out to him clearly and briefly the responsibilities which he is desirous of attaching to himself. By HENRY STEPHEN and HORACE MILLER, LL.B., Authors of "The County Council Compendium." Crown 8vo. In cloth, 2s. 6d.

THE COUNTY COUNCILS AND MUNICIPAL CORPORATIONS COM-PANION AND DIARY, STATISTICAL CHRONICLE AND LOCAL GOVERNMENT YEAR BOOK.—The most complete work of reference in connection with County and Borough Administration extant. Compiled and edited by Sir J. R. SOMERS VINE, F.S.S. Two Editions, with Diary three days to a page. No. 1 bound in cloth, lettered, 10s. 6d. No. 2, bound in crimson morocco, gilt edges, &c., and subscriber's name lettered on cover, 15s.

THE COUNTY COURTS ACT, 1888.—Queen's Printers' Copy, with an introduction indicating the leading alterations made by the Act, a Comprehensive Index, &c., &c., and the County Courts Admiralty Jurisdiction Acts, 1868 and 1869, with a separate Index, by R. T. HUNTER, Chief Clerk, County Court, Stockton-on-Tees. Second Edition. In boards, cloth back, 5s. The same may be had with the Act Interleaved for Notes. In boards, 6s.

THE COUNTY COURT RULES, 1889, with an Index to the Pages, Orders, Rules, Forms and Fees, an Alphabetical List of Forms (referring to page, order, and rule), and Tables showing the Fees and Costs on any given sum. By R. T. HUNTER, Chief Clerk, County Court, Stockton-on-Tees. In boards, 7s., or in roan, 10s. 6d. The same Index in separate form, in boards, 3s. 6d.

COSTS IN THE COUNTY COURT under the County Court Acts, 1888, and Rules of 1889 and 1892, with the Sections and Rules relating thereto and Precedents. By R. T. HUNTER, Chief Clerk, County Court, Stockton-on-Tees. Price 6s.

DEBTORS AND CREDITORS. — A Guide to the Proceedings for Recovery of Debt by Action in the County Courts or in the High Court, and the Administration of Insolvent Estates, showing the position of Debtors and Creditors under the various proceedings, including Private Arrangements between Debtors and Creditors, and particulars as to the Registration of Deeds under the Deeds of Arrangement Registration Act. Also a List of the County Courts in each County of England and Wales, giving the Bankruptcy Court to which each is attached and the name of the Official Receiver in Bankruptcy for the District. By ERNEST SAVILLE, of the Bankruptcy Department, Board of Trade. In cloth, 3s. 6d.

THE DEEDS OF ARRANGEMENT ACT, 1887, AND THE BANKRUPTCY (DISCHARGE AND CLOSURE) ACT, 1887, with Rules, Forms, and Scales of Fees prescribed thereunder; also with Notes and Index. By His Honour Judge CHALMERS and E. HOUGH, Inspector in Bankruptcy, Board of Trade. In boards, 2s. 6d. In cloth, 3s. 6d.

DUE DATE TABLES FOR ACCEPTING BILLS OF EXCHANGE. Compiled by HENRY BELL and JOHN MONTGOMERY, JR. These Tables are most useful to Bankers, Merchants, Manufacturers and others, are perpetually serviceable, and suffer no alteration from year to year. In cloth, 7s. 6d.

THE DUTIES OF EXECUTORS. By F. W. DENDY, Solicitor and Notary. Fifth Edition. Post free, 1s. 7d.

THE ELECTORAL BOUNDARIES OF THE UNITED KINGDOM, being Schedules 5, 6, and 7 of the Parliamentary Elections (Redistribution) Act, 1885. With Index. In boards, 2s. 6d.

THE ELECTRIC LIGHTING ACT, 1882, with Hints to Local Authorities, Explanatory Notes and Amended Rules of the Board of Trade, &c. By ARTHUR P. POLEY, B.A., of the Inner Temple, Barrister-at-Law, and FRANK DETHRIDGE. In cloth, 2s.

THE ENGLISH MUNICIPAL CODE, or the MUNICIPAL CORPORATIONS (Consolidation) ACT, 1882, with Statutes and Cases from 1882 to 1888, Notes, Comments, References, Statistical Appendix, and Voluminous Index. By Sir J. R. SOMERS VINE, F.S.S. Third Edition. In cloth, 7s. 6d.

ENGLISH MUNICIPAL INSTITUTIONS: THEIR GROWTH AND DEVELOPMENT STATISTICALLY ILLUSTRATED.—"A most useful and valuable work."—*Vide* Public Press. By Sir J. R. SOMERS VINE, F.S.S. Royal 8vo, cloth, bevelled boards, 10s. 6d.

THE FORM OF BILLS OF SALE UNDER THE BILLS OF SALE ACT (1878) AMENDMENT ACT, 1882. By STANLEY BUCKMASTER, M.A., of the Inner Temple, Barrister-at-Law. In cloth, 2s. 6d.

THE FRANCHISE ACTS, 1884-5, being the Representation of the People Act, 1884; Registration Act, 1885; Parliamentary Elections (Redistribution) Act, 1885, and Medical Relief Disqualification Removal Act, 1885, with Introduction and Notes. By MILES WALKER MATTINSON, Barrister-at-Law, Joint Author of "Mattinson and Macaskie on Corrupt Practices." In boards, 2s. 6d.

GENERAL RAILWAY ACTS, 1830-1884.—A Collection of the Public General Acts for the Regulation of Railways, including the Companies, Lands, and Railways Clauses Consolidation Acts. Fourteenth Edition, as amended to close of the Session, 1884. By JAS. BIGG, Esq. In cloth, 21s.

A GUIDE TO THE LAW AND PRACTICE OF PETTY SESSIONS, with the Summary Jurisdiction Act, 1879. By EDWARD T. AYERS, Solicitor and Late Assistant Clerk to Justices, Great Yarmouth. In cloth, 5s.

GUIDE TO THE LAW OF DISTRESS FOR RENT. A handbook for Landlords, Land Agents, Certified Bailiffs, and others. By R. T. HUNTER, Chief Clerk, County Court, Stockton-on-Tees. Fifth Edition. In cloth, 3s. 6d. net.

GUIDE TO THE PREPARATION OF BILLS OF COSTS (PRIDMORE'S), containing Practical Directions for Taxing Costs, and complete Precedents of Bills of Costs in all the Divisions, in conformity with the present Practice. Ninth Edition. By CHAS. W. SCOTT, one of the Principal Clerks in the Chancery Taxing Office, Royal Courts of Justice. In cloth, 25s.

A HANDBOOK OF THE LAW RELATING TO THE MANAGEMENT OF PARLIAMENTARY, COUNTY COUNCIL AND MUNICIPAL ELECTIONS. A statement of the Law relating to the Machinery of Elections. Second Edition. By H. STEPHEN, Barrister-at-Law. In cloth, 1s.

HANDBOOK TO THE PATENTS, DESIGNS AND TRADE-MARKS ACT, 1883, containing the Act and Rules, also an Explanatory and Practical Treatise thereon and the Procedure thereunder. For the use of Inventors, Manufacturers, &c., with a Copious Index to the Act and Rules. By BRISTOW HUNT, Consulting Patent Agent. In cloth, 5s.

HANDBOOK TO THE SMALL HOLDINGS ACT, 1892, and the Statutory provisions incorporated therein, with Notes and an Index. By HORACE E. MILLER, LL.B., Barrister-at-Law. In cloth, 2s. 6d.

HANDBOOK TO THE STAMP DUTIES, containing the Text of the Stamp Acts, 1891, and a complete Alphabetical Table of all documents liable to Stamp Duty, with an Index. By H. S. BOND, Esq., of the Solicitors' Department, Inland Revenue, Somerset House. Seventh Edition. Post free, 2s.

INDIAN EXCHANGE TABLES.—By J. I. BERRY. In cloth, 21s., or with Supplement, 25s.

SUPPLEMENT TO DITTO, 5s.
SECOND SUPPLEMENT TO DITTO, 5s.

INTEREST TABLES at the rate of two and three-quarters per cent. per annum on sums varying from £1 to £10,000 for all periods from 1 to 364 days, and from 1 to 12 months. Compiled by F. ALBAN BARRAUD, Solicitor. In cloth, 2s. 6d.

THE JOINT-STOCK COMPANIES PRACTICAL GUIDE. By HENRY HURRELL and CLARENDON G. HYDE, Barristers-at-Law. Invaluable to the Legal Profession and to Secretaries, Directors, Promoters and all other persons engaged in the formation or management of Joint Stock Companies. Fourth Edition. In cloth, 5s.

THE LAW AND PROCEDURE OF SUMMARY JUDGMENT ON SPECIALLY INDORSED WRIT, under Order XIV. By C. CAVANAGH, of the Middle Temple, Barrister-at-Law. In cloth, 5s. net.

THE LAW AND PRACTICE OF COPYHOLD ENFRANCHISEMENT AND COMMUTATION AND EXTINGUISHMENT OF MANORIAL IN-CIDENTS, UNDER THE COPYHOLD ACTS, 1841 to 1887, Consolidated, Tabulated and Arranged, with Practical Notes, Suggestions and Instructions; Tables of Valuation and Valuers' Allowance; and an Appendix of all the Forms. By W. STEPHEN TUNBRIDGE, Solicitor (Honours). In cloth, 6s.

LAW AND PRACTICE OF REGISTRATION OF DEEDS IN THE COUNTY OF MIDDLESEX under the Middlesex Deeds Acts containing the full texts of the Acts, Rules and Fee Order with notes, instructions, precedents of Memorials, &c., by C. FORTESCUE-BRICKDALE, of Lincoln's Inn, Barrister-at-Law. In cloth, 3s. 3d.

THE LAW OF BUILDING AND ENGINEERING CONTRACTS and of the Duties and Liabilities of Engineers, Architects, Surveyors and Valuers. A Treatise with an Appendix of Precedents, annotated by means of Reference to the Text and to Contracts in use, and an Appendix of Unreported Cases on Building and Engineering Contracts. By ALFRED A. HUDSON, of the Inner Temple, Barrister-at-Law. In cloth, 36s., or for Cash with Order, including Carriage, 30s.

THE LAW OF DIRECTORS AND OFFICERS OF JOINT STOCK COMPANIES, their Powers, Duties and Liabilities. By HENRY HURRELL, of the Middle Temple, and CLARENDON G. HYDE, of the Middle Temple, Barristers-at-Law. Second Edition. In cloth, 5s; and, as a Supplement, a Treatise on the Directors' Liability Act, 1890. Post free, 7d.

THE LAW OF MERCANTILE AGENTS; or, THE FACTORS' ACT, 1889. By M. MOLONEY, Barrister-at-law. In cloth boards, post free, 1s. 7d.

THE LAW OF MERCHANT SHIPPING AND FREIGHT, with Tables of Cases, Forms and Complete Index. By J. T. FOARD, of the Inner Temple, Barrister-at-Law. Royal 8vo. In half-calf, 21s.

THE LAW OF RATES AND CHARGES ON RAILWAYS AND CANALS. Synopsis of the Railway and Canal Traffic Act, 1888. By PERCY GYE and THOS. WAGHORN, of the Inner Temple, Barristers-at-Law. In boards, 2s. In cloth, 3s.

THE LAW RELATING TO BETTING, TIME BARGAINS AND GAMING, including the Law relating to Stakeholders, Stewards, the Winners of Races, &c.; Stock Exchange Transactions, Sale of Bank Shares, &c., Lotteries, Gaming Houses, Betting Houses, Places and Lists, and Licensed Premises. By GEORGE HERBERT STUTFIELD, and HENRY S. CAUTLEY, Barristers-at-Law. Third Edition, revised and enlarged. In boards, 2s. 6d.

THE LAW RELATING TO CORRUPT PRACTICES AT PARLIAMENTARY, MUNICIPAL AND OTHER ELECTIONS, AND THE PRACTICE OF ELECTION PETITIONS, with an Appendix of Statutes, Rules and Forms. By MILES WALKER MATTINSON and STUART CUNNINGHAM MACASKIE, of Gray's Inn, Barristers-at-Law. Third Edition. In cloth, 10s.

MANUAL OF HYDROLOGY.—By N. BEARDMORE, C.E. In cloth, 24s.

THE MARRIED WOMEN'S PROPERTY ACT, 1882.—A concise Treatise, showing the effect of this Act upon the existing Law. By THOMAS BARRETT-LENNARD, of the Middle Temple, Barrister-at-Law. Second Edition. In stiff boards, 1s. 6d.

MANUAL OF THEATRICAL LAW, containing instructions for Licensing Theatres and Music Halls, and Chapter on the Law of Contracts between Actors and Managers, &c., &c. By CLARENCE HAMLYN, of the Middle Temple, Barrister-at-Law. In cloth. 5s.

MERCATOR'S BUSINESS AND SOCIAL TELEGRAPHIC POCKET CODE.— Compiled by a practical Telegraphist. In cloth, 5s. net.

THE ORGANIZATION OF A SOLICITOR'S OFFICE, being a reprint (with revisions) of a Series of Articles contributed to the "Solicitors' Journal," by EDWARD F. TURNER, Solicitor. Third Edition. In cloth, 7s. 6d.

THE POSITION IN LAW OF WOMEN.—Showing how it differs from that of Men, and the effect of the Married Women's Property Act, 1882. By THOMAS BARRETT-LENNARD, of the Middle Temple, Barrister-at-Law. In cloth, 6s.

PRACTICAL HINTS ON THE PREPARATION AND REGISTRATION of Joint Stock Companies' Forms, with Precedents, Tables of Fees and Stamp Duties and an Index. Post free, 1s. 7d.

PRACTICAL SUGGESTIONS ON THE PREPARATION AND REGISTRA- TION OF DEEDS, and other documents at the various Public Offices, with Tables of Fees and an Index. Post free, 1s. 7d.

THE PRACTICE OF THE LAND REGISTRY UNDER THE TRANSFER OF LAND ACT, 1862, with such portions of the Rules as are now in force, and General Instructions, Notes, Forms and Precedents. By CHARLES FORTESCUE-BRICKDALE, B.A., of Lincoln's Inn, Barrister, Assisting Barrister to the Land Registry, and Author of "Registration of Title in Prussia, &c., &c. In cloth, 3s. 6d.

PRINCIPLES AND PRECEDENTS OF MODERN CONVEYANCING.— A Concise Exposition of the Draftsman's Art, with a Series of Forms framed in accordance with the Acts of 1881 and 1882. By C. CAVANAGH, B.A., LL.B. (Lond.), of the Middle Temple and Northern Circuit, Barrister-at-Law; Author of "The Law of Money Securities." In cloth, 15s.

RAILWAYS IN SCOTLAND, 1845-1873.—The General Acts for the Regulation of Railways in Scotland, including the Companies, Lands, and Railways Clauses (Scotland) Acts, complete to the close of 1873, and a copious Index. A Supplement to the General Railway Acts. 12mo. In cloth (1873), 5s.

SHORT AND CONCISE PRECEDENTS OF THE CLAUSES MOST GENERALLY IN USE IN FARMING AGREEMENTS, with complete Forms of Agreements, Dissertations, and Full Notes, and a Table of Contents. By J. W. JEUDWINE, of Lincoln's Inn, Barrister-at-Law, In boards, 2s.

THE SOLICITORS' DIARY, ALMANAC, LEGAL DIGEST, AND DIRECTORY.—The Edition for 1893 is the 49th year of publication of this important Annual, which is now universally recognised as the most useful Legal Diary published. Published annually in October. Prices: 3s. 6d., 5s., 6s., and 8s. 6d., according to diary space and binding.

THE SOLICITORS' POCKET BOOK.—In leather tuck 2s. 6d., roan wallet, 4s. 6d. ; and Russia wallet, 7s. 6d

STANDING ORDERS.—The Standing Orders of the Lords and Commons relative to Private Bills, with Appendix. Published at the close of each Session. In cloth, 5s.

THE SUMMARY JURISDICTION ACT, 1884, with Notes.—A Supplement to Ayers' "Guide to the Law and Practice of Petty Sessions." By EDWARD T. AYERS, Solicitor. In boards, 2s.

A SUPPLEMENT TO THE THIRTEENTH EDITION OF THE GENERAL RAILWAY ACTS, containing the Enactments affecting Railways in England and Ireland passed in Sessions 1875 to 1883. By JAS. BIGG, Esq. In cloth, 5s.

TABLE OF CORRUPT AND ILLEGAL PRACTICES WHICH VITIATE THE ELECTION. By M. W. MATTINSON and S. C. MACASKIE, Barristers-at-Law. On linen-lined card. Prices: 1 copy, 2d. ; 50 copies, 6s. ; 100 copies, 10s. May also be had printed on stout cardboard 11 by 17, suitable for affixing to the walls of Committee Rooms. Price 6d. each.

TABLE OF FEES, CHARGES AND EXPENSES, AND COURT FEES, UNDER THE LAW OF DISTRESS AMENDMENT ACT, 1888. Stamp Duty on Appraisement, Fees Chargeable by High Bailiffs, &c. By R. T. HUNTER, Chief Clerk, County Court, Stockton-on-Tees. Mounted on linen and folded in cloth case, 1s. 6d.

TABLES FOR THE IMMEDIATE CONVERSION OF PRODUCTS INTO INTEREST AT TWENTY-NINE RATES, viz.:—From one to eight per cent. inclusive, &c., &c. By A. CROSBIE and W. C. LAW. Second Edition. Improved and enlarged. In roan, 12s. 6d.

THE TIME TABLES FOR THE HIGH COURT OF JUSTICE AND FOR THE COUNTY COURT. Revised and Corrected up to May, 1884. By J. W. JEUDWINE, Barrister-at-Law. Second Edition. In cloth, 1s.

VADE MECUM TO THE BILLS OF EXCHANGE, BANKRUPTCY, AND BILLS OF SALE ACTS, comprising a complete List of Cases appended to the various sections of the Acts to which they respectively refer. By SYLVAIN MAYER, B.A., Ph.D., of the Middle Temple, Barrister-at-Law. In cloth, 1s.

WATERLOW'S BIJOU AND CONDENSED DIARIES. Published in October. These elegant and useful Pocket Diaries are issued in two sizes, series Y, 3¾ by 2½, series Z, 4½ by 2¾, artistically printed in two colours on metallic paper, and can be had in paper covers at 1s. 6d. and 1s. 9d. each, and covered in silk at 2s. and 2s. 6d. each, or in roan, morocco, Russia, or crocodile wallets, from 5s. each.

WATERLOW'S SCRIBBLING DIARY. Foolscap folio, 6 days on a page interleaved, strong paper cover, 1s.; ditto 3 days, 1s. 6d.: ditto two days, ¼ bound cloth, 3s. ; ditto one day, 5s.

SECOND EDITION.

Dedicated by permission to the Right Hon. The President of the Local Government Board.

THE COUNTY COUNCIL COMPENDIUM,

OR DIGEST OF THE MUNICIPAL CORPORATION ACT, 1882, THE COUNTY ELECTORS ACT, 1888, AND LOCAL GOVERNMENT ACT, 1888.

BEING A TREATISE ON THE ABOVE STATUTES AND OTHERS RE-ENACTED THEREIN, WITH COPIOUS NOTES AND APPENDICES.

BY

HENRY STEPHEN,

AND

HORACE E. MILLER, LL.B.,

OF THE MIDDLE TEMPLE, BARRISTERS-AT-LAW.

In Cloth 21s., or for cash with order, 18s.

OPINIONS OF THE PRESS.

" **Law Times** " says :—" Among the expositions of the general effect of the new legislation it stands high for clearness of thought and expression. It is a well-conceived and well-arranged piece of timely work. The index appears comprehensive and excellent, and reflects great credit on its compilers."

" **Law Journal** " says :—" The Compendium appears to deserve its name, and to give an admirable general idea of the local constitution of the land, together with material for obtaining more minute information."

" **Solicitors' Journal** " says :—" The first chapter contains a terse and well-digested summary of the leading changes effected by the Act. The authors then proceed to deal with the constitution and election of county councils. The information under this head is full and clearly arranged under sub-headings."

" **Saturday Review** " says :—" A lucid and able digest of the County Electors Act, the Local Government Act, and the Municipal Corporations Act, 1882. The book, in fact, is a concise treatise on the enormous changes in local government that will come into operation in April, and a handy volume of reference for officials and electors. The magnitude of the new scheme of Local Government is unfolded with admirable clearness and cumulative effect."

" **County Gentleman** " says :—" The first chapter of the 'County Council Compendium' gives us, in admirable concise and intelligible terms, a very clear idea of the organic changes which the new legislation will effect in matters of local administration throughout England and Wales. It is, indeed, difficult to over-estimate the value of a work which reflects additional credit upon its authors for the promptitude of its appearance, and for the general simple and non-technical language which will render it available for the practical guidance of lay readers."

" **Daily News** " says :—" A complete and useful treatise upon the Local Government Acts."

Crown 8vo. In Cloth, Two Shillings and Sixpence.

THE

COUNTY COUNCILLOR'S

VADE-MECUM.

This handbook deals with the powers and duties of County Councils in a way which, it is believed, is specially adapted for general readers.

BY

HENRY STEPHEN,

Of the Middle Temple, Barrister-at-Law. Editor of the 9th Edition of " Stephen's Commentaries ;"

AND

HORACE E. MILLER, LL.B.,

Of the Middle Temple, Barrister-at-Law.

OPINIONS OF THE PRESS.

"**Law Times**" says—"This task they proceed to essay in a neat little book of some seventy pages, with clear and perspicuous writing and arrangement, ... We think well of the Vade-Mecum."

"**Law Journal**" says—"Mr. Stephen produces, jointly with Mr. Miller, a little book which may be presented to a newly-elected councillor as a pleasing form of congratulation. The 'Vade-Mecum' seems to carry out its object."

"**Isle of Ely and Wisbech Advertiser**" says—"The avoidance of technical language and details, and at the same time a careful attention to accuracy in putting the Act into language easily understood, will make it peculiarly reliable to the general reader."

SECOND EDITION.

Revised and Enlarged, with additional Precedents, and an Index of Forms.

THE AGRICULTURAL HOLDINGS (ENGLAND) ACT, 1883,

WITH

NOTES AND FORMS,

AND

A SUMMARY OF THE PROCEDURE.

BY

J. W. JEUDWINE,

OF LINCOLN'S INN, BARRISTER-AT-LAW.

In Cloth, 3s. 6d.

Supplement to Jeudwine's Treatise on the Agricultural Holdings Act, 1883.

SHORT AND CONCISE PRECEDENTS OF THE

CLAUSES MOST GENERALLY IN USE

IN

FARMING AGREEMENTS.

WITH

COMPLETE FORMS OF AGREEMENTS, DISSERTATIONS, AND FULL NOTES, AND A TABLE OF CONTENTS.

BY

J. W. JEUDWINE,

OF LINCOLN'S INN, BARRISTER-AT-LAW.

In Boards, 2s.

WATERLOW & SONS LIMITED,

FIFTH EDITION, GREATLY ENLARGED.

A GUIDE

TO THE

LAW OF DISTRESS
FOR RENT,

INCLUDING THE

STATUTES THEREON, FROM 1266 TO 1888,

WITH NOTES AND REFERENCES,

AND THE

RULES, TABLE OF FEES AND FORMS UNDER THE
NEW ACT,

TABLES OF STEPS IN A DISTRESS,

ALSO

REPLEVIN, RECOVERY OF POSSESSION OF TENEMENTS,
THE APPRAISERS' AND AUCTIONEERS' ACTS, &c.

AND A

TABLE OF FEES UNDER THE SHERIFFS' ACT, 1887.

BY

R. T. HUNTER,

*Chief Clerk, County Court, Stockton-on-Tees, Author of "The County Courts Act, 1888,"
and Joint Author of "An Index to the County Court Rules, 1886," &c.*

In Cloth, 3s. 6d. net.

TABLE OF FEES, CHARGES AND EXPENSES, AND COURT FEES,
UNDER THE LAW OF DISTRESS AMENDMENT ACT, 1888.

Stamp Duty on Appraisement, Fees Chargeable by High Bailiffs, &c.

By R. T. Hunter, Chief Clerk, County Court, Stockton-on-Tees.

Mounted on linen and folded in cloth case, 1s. 6d.

www.ingramcontent.com/pod-product-compliance
Lightning Source LLC
Chambersburg PA
CBHW032018010726
47493CB00007B/2464